D1176498

THE
GRAVEYARD
GANG

THE
GRAVEYARD
GANG

JAMES DUFFY

CHARLES SCRĪBNER'S SONS • NEW YORK
Maxwell Macmillan Canada • Toronto
Maxwell Macmillan International
New York • Oxford • Singapore • Sydney

Charles Scribner's Sons Books for Young Readers
Macmillan Publishing Company
866 Third Avenue, New York, NY 10022

Maxwell Macmillan Canada, Inc.
1200 Eglinton Avenue East, Suite 200
Don Mills, Ontario M3C 3N1

Macmillan Publishing Company is part of
the Maxwell Communication Group of Companies.

First edition   10 9 8 7 6 5 4 3 2 1

Printed in the United States of America

Library of Congress Cataloging-in-Publication Data
Duffy, James, date.
The Graveyard Gang / James Duffy. — 1st ed.   p.   cm.
Summary: During the summer after seventh grade, life in a small New Hampshire town improves for Amy, when new friendships help her deal with her father's death, her mother's emotional problems, and the accusation that she killed a local boy.
ISBN 0-684-19449-X
[1. Interpersonal relations—Fiction. 2. Emotional problems—Fiction.
3. New Hampshire—Fiction. 4. Mystery and detective stories.]   I. Title.
PZ7.D87814Gr 1993   [Fic]—dc20   92-30990

For Amanda

THE
GRAVEYARD
GANG

·1·

The sun slipped behind the trees in the old graveyard beyond the baseball field. The annual softball game between the parents and the school teams was in the last inning. The teachers were shaking hands with the eighth graders, who were going off in September to the regional high school. They signed the yearbooks and told the eighth graders to come back and visit when they had time. Then they finished their hamburgers and Cokes and, when no one was looking, sneaked away to begin *their* vacations—a whole summer without kids.

Amy wondered how she would feel next year when she graduated from Bromfield and had to leave the familiar wooden grade school. She supposed she would be scared. She didn't know anyone in the other three towns that shared the regional high school. And it was almost an hour's ride in the school bus—when it didn't snow—to Norton Falls. The bus started in Wingate and made its way twenty miles through Winthrop and Coldstream. Her brother, Stephen, said it had been like a trip to the moon and back. He was lucky. When Mom and Paul found out the high school wasn't much good, they took Stephen out at midyear and sent him off to boarding school in Massachusetts.

They wouldn't send her off, Amy knew. Mom said she didn't believe in boarding school for girls. Paul didn't say anything. She was Mom's daughter, not his, and he didn't meddle in children's business.

The long shadows turned into dusk. The first mosquitoes of the season ventured out of the woods. Amy looked around the field to see who was left. Across the way Sandy Prescott was sitting on the back steps of the school building. She waved to Amy. Something told Amy she couldn't let the day end when the picnic was over. If she did it would be a long, lonely summer in the big white house. She had to hold on to this day an hour longer, just long enough to make plans, any kind of plans, for company.

She strolled over to Sandy, who smiled. "Hi, Sandy," she said.

"Hi," Sandy responded. She moved over.

"What are you doing this summer?"

"I'm staying with Agatha Bates while Mom and Kate are in Boston."

"They're going to Boston? I used to live just outside."

"Mom is going to cooking school," Sandy said. "We're taking over the old inn."

Amy asked, "You're not going, too?"

"No. It's better if I finish school here. I'll be staying with Mrs. Bates until Christmas. You know, she lives over on the edge of the soccer field, beyond the graveyard."

Amy knew the old graveyard. She had gone there a couple of times to sit by herself on the wall and eat her lunch. It was in the trees between the baseball field and the lake. It wasn't used anymore. The last marker was almost a hundred years old, they said. Most of the slate and granite headstones had fallen over or worn away. Chipmunks ran along the wall, chattering at intruders. "Isn't it scary to live that close to the graveyard?" she asked.

"I don't think so. You can't even see it. Well, I'll head for home." Sandy stood up.

"I was wondering," Amy almost shouted, before Sandy could get away, "if some of us could do something together this summer."

Sandy stopped. "Like what?"

"Like a club, maybe." Amy couldn't think of anything else. In the books she read girls were always starting clubs and having adventures. Of course, none of them lived in Wingate, New Hampshire, year-round population under two thousand.

"What kind of club?"

"We could decide that when we get together," Amy said bravely. "Why don't we get Wilma and Cathy and go talk about it in the graveyard?"

"Now?"

"Sure, right now."

"It'll be getting dark soon," Sandy objected.

"We can walk home together."

Sandy thought it over for a moment. "Okay," she said.

·2·

"This place gives me the creeps," Wilma Hughes complained.

"What did you want to talk to us about, Amy?" Cathy Cameron said. "It's going to be dark pretty soon."

"I thought we could start a club, a sort of secret club, just the four of us."

"What kind of club?" Cathy asked suspiciously.

"Just a club for ourselves. We can decide later. We can meet here after supper and plan things to do."

When no one responded, Amy's voice rose as she continued. "Well, there's nothing else to do up here, is there? You can't even get television, it's so streaky. What are we going to do all summer except wait for school to open in September?"

Cathy slapped a mosquito on her knee. "It's buggy out here."

"I still don't know what we're going to do," Wilma complained. "Will someone please tell me what we're going to do, so we can leave? I'm scared."

Amy had to come up with something fast. She couldn't tell them she hated Wingate, that she didn't know how she could get through the summer here, where the big event of the week was a soft-ice-cream cone at the general store.

"Well," she stammered, "we could start a summer camp for little kids—give them lunch, take them swimming, and stuff like that. We could put up a tent right here in the school yard. My brother has a tent he never used."

Cathy made a face. "I have to baby-sit my brother at home. That's enough for me."

"How about cleaning houses, then?" Amy said. "We could do odd jobs and wash windows."

Cathy and Wilma looked at Sandy, who hadn't said anything. "I don't think we'd do much business," Sandy said at last.

Wilma agreed. "My mother does all that kind of work. If she needs help, she makes me do it."

"What about the lodge in Puckett's Notch?" Amy asked in desperation. "They must need something done over there with all the summer people they get. We could caddie or clean up or cut grass."

Sandy showed some interest. "I'd like that," she said. "I'd really like to go someplace different and see some people I don't know. And I'd like to learn something. But they probably wouldn't hire thirteen-year-olds. I think there's a law that says they can't."

"I'll find out," Amy said, "and report back. Agreed?"

Sandy and Cathy and Wilma nodded.

"We'll meet here Wednesday right after supper," Amy suggested. "About seven o'clock?"

Sandy and Cathy and Wilma nodded again. They stood to leave.

"Well, well, look who's here," a harsh voice called out from behind them. "It's the graveyard gang."

The girls turned back toward the cemetery. It was Donald

Jenkins. Amy had seen him in town. The kids called him Bigmouth. Perry Whitman was with him. They were in their swimming trunks on the way home from the beach, taking the shortcut through the cemetery. Donald leaped over the stone wall. "Come on, Perry. Let's let the graveyard girls get on with their digging."

Perry Whitman hadn't budged. For another minute or so he stood, silent, in the gloom of the graveyard, staring at the girls with dark, sullen eyes. Then he walked slowly to the wall and stepped over. He turned to stare again before he followed Bigmouth across the field.

"That guy Perry gives me the creeps," Cathy said. "He never opens his mouth. He just follows Bigmouth around like a zombie. The fool and the ghoul, my mother calls them. Let's wait until they cross the field before we leave."

· 3 ·

"Could we meet somewhere else?" Wilma complained as the girls started home. "The graveyard really scares me. We could meet at my house and have popcorn."

"We'll take a vote next time," Sandy assured her. "How about that? Do we meet again on Wednesday?"

"I'll talk to my stepfather about the lodge," Amy said. "He handles some investments for them."

"Yeah, sure," Cathy said. She and Wilma headed down Main Street.

Amy and Sandy turned in the other direction, toward Old Winthrop Road, single file, Sandy walking ahead. No wonder I don't have any friends, and everyone in the seventh grade thinks I'm snooty, Amy thought. Why did she have to mention Paul and his investment business? She sounded like a rich kid. From now on, she would keep her mouth shut.

A car sped up behind them and then slammed on its brakes. The horn blared out. Amy scrambled into a ditch. "Watch out, Princess, or you won't get home to the palace. You're supposed to walk on the other side, *facing* traffic." Rock music poured from the car as it took off down the road. It turned down a rutted lane at the Whitman mailbox.

"It's Bigmouth, taking his friend Perry home," Sandy said. "His father lets him have the car now."

"Does he bother you and your sister?" Amy asked.

"Not really. They say he was an awful kid in elementary school. He was held back twice, so he was bigger than the other kids. He and Perry are loners. He's sixteen or seventeen now. Cathy knows him pretty well—he lives next door to her, and she says he's not so bad."

They had come to the dirt road where Sandy lived. "I'll see you Wednesday," Sandy said. "Good luck with the lodge."

"Do you want me to stop for you?" Amy asked.

"I'll be at Agatha Bates's house. We're doing the kitchen over. We're painting the cupboards right now."

A quarter of a mile farther on, just over the hill, Amy reached her driveway. The big aluminum mailbox, with ABBOTT/BRUCE in plain black letters on the side, still looked new. So did the asphalt drive curving up to the house, known as the palace to the kids at school. The house wasn't any palace. It was just a big house, probably the biggest in Wingate, where most of the houses were sort of ordinary and small. Wingate wasn't what you'd call a rich town. Mom was always fussing that she couldn't find anything she needed in the general store. Once a week she and Amy drove to the little mall in Coldstream to do their shopping at the Big Value store, which wasn't much bigger than the general store. Mom hadn't been happy about anything in Wingate—the school, the stores, the streaky television, the snow, the black flies. "We're living on the edge of nowhere," she kept saying to Paul.

Part of the problem was that Mom didn't have any friends in Wingate. More and more she sat all day and half the night in her studio making greeting cards, which she shipped off to a company in St. Louis.

She'd gotten the idea that people in Wingate thought she was strange when she went into the library to ask for books the librarian had never heard of and when she mailed a package second-class airmail to friends in Europe. "They seemed to think it was disloyal for me to send things out of the country," she complained. Afterward, she bought her own stamps and weighed the packages and mailed them in the mailbox in Coldstream when she went to shop.

A few times last year Amy had invited classmates home after school. Mom had fussed over them, chattering away while she gave them cake and milk, talking too fast, trying to make conversation about school and their parents and so on. The girls wandered around the house counting the rooms, and went away and never asked Amy to come visit them. After a while Amy caught on that the kids only came to see her "palace" and the crazy people who lived in it. They didn't have any reason to come back. Amy stopped asking. In the spring Mom went into a deep depression, the way she had when Amy's dad died, and Paul took her back to the hospital outside of Boston.

Crutch was under the kitchen table waiting for her, his gray snout pointing toward the door. His tail thumped the floor in pleasure. Amy knelt under the table to hug him. She rubbed her face in Crutch's soft black fur. Crutch had come with the house. He showed up, limping, a week after they'd moved in, a big black stray with a white bib and four white feet. Stephen said he needed a crutch, and the name stuck.

He became Amy's dog. She was the one who fed him, brushed him, talked to him, and walked him down to the river at the bottom of the meadow. Crutch was her only real friend.

·4·

Paul turned his chair away from the computer worktable. A steady stream of figures poured across the screen. "Yes, Amy?" he asked politely. He reached around to push a button. The screen went blank. Amy understood that she wasn't supposed to bother Paul in the morning, but today the study door had been half open.

Paul wasn't such a bad guy. He probably just wasn't meant to be a dad, or at least not a dad to someone else's kids. Amy wasn't sure that he was even meant to be married. Sometimes when Mom was shouting at Paul, she'd say, "Why didn't you just leave us be? We could have made it without you."

Stephen had tried to explain to Amy once how Mom was disappointed in life. He could remember back to their dad and mom better than Amy could. Her memories of her father were of a big, broad man who swept her into his arms when he came home in the evenings and talked silly talk. There was usually something from the office in his pocket, a big paper clip, a little magnifying glass, a rubber stamp.

No silly talk ever came from Mom that Amy could recall. Right after Amy was born, according to Stephen, Mom took up painting and gave up kids and house and husband for her

11

art. It was something called therapy. Amy remembered the baby-sitters she'd had and the play schools, and not much about Mom. Mom wasn't a very good painter, Stephen said, and after a while Dad made the mistake of telling her that, suggesting that she ought to look after her family more. Mom cut up all her paintings and threw away her brushes and paints, and told Dad she would never forgive him.

Amy wondered if Mom had forgiven Dad by the time he was killed when a teenager in a stolen pickup ran into him at the intersection down the street from their house. It was about a year later when she married Dad's partner, Paul Bruce. "I think he felt bad about Dad," Stephen said, "and figured he had to look after Mom or something. Who knows? Maybe he figured it was time to get married, and Mom saved him the trouble of looking around."

After a while, Mom couldn't deal with depression and went into the hospital. When she came home Paul bought the big house in Wingate and talked Mom into bringing the family up from Boston to live there. That sure had been a mistake.

Amy was deep in her thoughts when she realized that Paul had spoken to her again.

He was looking down at the complicated gold watch he always wore. If you pushed this button or that button, it would tell you what time it was anywhere in the world. Paul had promised Stephen one just like it if he helped him this summer.

"I'm sorry," she said. "I had an idea Saturday, but now I'm not sure it was such a hot idea. I'm sorry I bothered you."

"Sit down. You didn't bother me. Why don't you tell me, anyway."

The old-timers in Wingate had nothing but contempt for

the exclusive Spruce Tree Lodge. In the summer expensive sports cars and big station wagons full of rich kids in alligator shirts and hundred-dollar running shoes sped through Wingate on their way to Puckett's Notch. In the winter the cars came racing by again, usually without the kids and with skis strapped on their roofs. Once in a while the drivers stopped at the general store for suntan lotion or a soda, but usually they drove through town without slowing down.

Was that where she wanted to work this summer? Amy asked herself. The kids already thought she was a snob.

"Well, after the picnic Saturday," Amy began, "some other kids and I decided to start a club. It was my idea, mostly, because there's not going to be much to do around here in the summer. I thought the club could ask at the lodge if they could use some help, cleaning up, lawn work, whatever."

"That's a good idea," Paul said. "I understand they're always short of help up there."

"We know we're not old enough to be regular help. Sandy says you have to be older to have a real job."

"That sounds about right," Paul agreed.

"We don't know if we could be paid or not. We don't want to work for nothing, I guess."

"No, that would be foolish," Paul commented. "People who work hard expect to be paid, even if it's not always in money."

"Then this morning," Amy went on, "it didn't seem like such a hot idea. It rains a lot up at the lodge."

"That's what they say around here, don't they? Don't believe that kind of talk, Amy. It rains precisely as much— or as little—as it does here. It will probably be a sunny, dry summer."

"How do you know?" Amy asked.

"That's the long-term forecast by the weather bureau. Believe it or not, I have to keep track of things like the weather. It has a small effect on what happens on the market. Hot, sticky weather, for example, makes people nervous. That could make the market fluctuate, go up and down, a bit more than usual."

That was pretty interesting. If Paul said it was going to be a good summer, it was almost certain to be a good summer. Paul didn't make many mistakes, Stephen had said. "Except for Mom," he'd added.

"Well, we could ask at least," Amy said. "Who's the person we should talk to? I'll ride my bike over to the lodge to talk to him."

"It's Bob Harlow. We're having a drink this afternoon. Business talk. Come on along. We'll talk your business first." The watch on Paul's wrist beeped once. After ten seconds it beeped and didn't stop. Paul pushed a button. "I have to make a call. All right if we go to the lodge about four-thirty?"

·5·

"What are you going to say to Bob Harlow?" Paul asked Amy as they drove toward Puckett's Notch. "You should have it straight in your mind before you see him. That helps him *and* you. I suspect the possibility of hiring someone like you hasn't occurred to him. He relies on his permanent staff. I've noticed it is pretty messy by the pool sometimes, towels scattered all over and dirty glasses on the tables. That makes a bad impression. And sometimes there isn't enough staff at the entrance to take care of the luggage. The cars get backed up. The room maids could probably use a helper to take the dirty linen to the laundry; the grounds keepers can always use an extra hand in the summer months."

This was a side of Paul that Amy hadn't seen before. Imagine noticing that it was messy at the pool and the guests had to wait for someone to take their luggage. "The lodge is pretty fancy, isn't it?" she said.

"It's overpriced, so I suppose that makes it fancy. I doubt that the guests get their money's worth."

"Why do they come here, then?" Amy asked. "It's buried out in nowhere, Mom says."

"Like us, too, is that right, Amy?" Paul laughed. "Because

15

it's beautiful, the air is fresh, and it's hard to get to. That makes it exclusive."

Mr. Harlow took them to a terrace outside the lounge. At the bottom of the slope was an enormous swimming pool with a high board and a low board and a tall, twisting slide. Amy couldn't see any towels lying around. Beyond the pool a lake reached up to the edge of Mount something-or-other. No motorboats, she noticed. A couple of sailboats, paddleboats, rowboats, and canoes, yes, but no noisy motorboats.

"Amy has something she wants to talk to you about, don't you, Amy?"

Amy's attention was pulled away from the pool and lake. "Oh, I'm sorry. I was thinking how beautiful it is here. I mean, I've never seen such a lovely place. It must be hard to keep it up." That ought to please Paul. Mr. Harlow was smiling in agreement.

"We try to do that," he said. "It's difficult sometimes. A few of our guests think that because they pay a lot to stay here, they can behave in rather sloppy ways."

Amy realized that Mr. Harlow had talked to Paul about his problems. "Maybe it's because it's their vacation time, sir," she said.

"You're probably right there," Mr. Harlow agreed.

"But it must make a lot of work for you. Extra work, I mean, cleaning up."

"It does, Amy, it really does. It's a smart daughter you have here, Paul. Will you take her into the business along with Stephen?"

"I will someday. First, she wants to take over the Spruce Tree Lodge. Why don't you tell Mr. Harlow what you have in mind, Amy?"

16

Amy made her pitch. Now that Paul had prepared the way, it was easy. She explained to Mr. Harlow how convenient it would be for his people to have her and a couple of hardworking friends around to do odd jobs, to fill in and back up the regular staff.

The manager listened carefully. When she'd finished, Mr. Harlow said, "Congratulations. You're a born salesperson. You'll have your first million by the time you're ready to vote. Right, Paul?"

"If she gets off to a good start here, I'm sure she will."

"I'm convinced," Mr. Harlow said. "Do you want to start on Saturday, Amy? It's turnover day. A lot of people leave and others arrive. You'll get a good taste of the hotel business, and we'll see if you measure up. I'll have Charlene look after you. She's in charge of staff. Now, Paul, you said you wanted to make some changes in our portfolio. Why don't you take a look around the hotel and grounds, Amy?"

We haven't finished quite yet, Amy thought. Paul said the lodge would have to pay Amy and her friends in some way. "Speak right up, if Harlow doesn't mention it," he'd said.

Amy spoke up. "I don't think we can help you unless we get paid. Not much, because we're young and inexperienced, but something."

Harlow slapped his thigh. "I was waiting to see if you would bring that up. Payment, yes, indeed. Let me see. What did you have in mind? It's impossible for us to put you on regular salary. Against the law. You'll pick up some tips, I suppose, but not many. The regular staff has a right to them. And I can't let you use the pool or the tennis courts. I'd have some of the guests on my back."

"Gee, I don't know," Amy said when Mr. Harlow had exhausted the possibilities.

17

"What do you think, Paul? Any ideas on how we can pay the kids."

"You can have one of your cars pick them up and bring them home every day. And feed them. Your company owns the most elegant hotel in Boston. Why not give them a week down there at the end of the season? I'm sure some of their parents would chaperone them."

"Done!" Mr. Harlow said. "You go talk it over with your club. Let Charlene Spence know your decision. Wednesdays off. That's usually a dull day for some reason. Okay?"

"Okay," Amy said.

·6·

Amy sat on the stone wall of the graveyard, waiting for the rest of the club. She had pushed her new Italian ten-speed bike into the shadows. She hoped they wouldn't see it; it was no time to show off. The next time she would walk. She had put on her oldest pair of jeans, but they still looked pretty new. Last fall Mom had piled Amy into her car for a shopping weekend in Boston. The trunk had been full when they got back.

Two girls came across the field. Amy squinted. It was Cathy and Wilma. Wilma was waving her arms, complaining about something, Amy was sure. Whiny Wilma, the kids called her. Nothing seemed to go right for Wilma.

"Hi," Amy said. "Where's Sandy?"

"Right here," a voice said. It was Sandy coming out of the graveyard in back of her. "I've been over at Agatha's."

"I think we have jobs at the Spruce Tree Lodge if you want them," Amy began. She was very careful *not* to say that she had gotten them jobs.

"Yeah?" Cathy said. "That's pretty good. I didn't think they'd be interested in anyone from Wingate. Dad says they bring their own people in, college kids and fancy chefs from New York."

19

"I don't know about that," Amy said carefully. It was clear the lodge was a sore point with the people in Wingate. "I guess they can use some general help."

"Like what?" Wilma demanded. "I'm not going to carry any rich person's suitcase. They can carry their own luggage."

"That's dumb, Wilma," Sandy said. "If you take a job, you have to do what they tell you. I can think of worse things than carrying suitcases. You might get a tip. Isn't that right, Amy?"

"Maybe, but we have to be careful. Mr. Harlow said the regulars expect the big tips. But you might get some tips. What they want us to do are fill-in and help-out jobs. We'd be a backup staff, he said."

"My mother said she couldn't drive me over to the Spruce Tree Lodge and back every day," Wilma interrupted.

"We could have a car pool, I think," Cathy said. "Would she do that?"

"I don't think so," Wilma said. "She doesn't think much of the whole idea. Maybe if Dad was around . . ."

"Where's your dad?" Amy asked without thinking.

Wilma was silent.

"Her parents are divorced," Cathy explained for Wilma. "She lives with her mother. You have to talk about it, Wilma. Lots of kids have parents who are separated, right here in town. You know that."

I should set something straight, too, Amy thought. She had never talked about her father at school.

"My dad's dead, Wilma," she said. "He was killed in a car accident."

"Oh," Wilma said, at once interested and sympathetic. "We didn't know that, did we, Cathy?"

20

Cathy shook her head. "I'm sorry, Amy."

"Look, we don't need a carpool," Amy explained. "They'll pick us up and bring us back. That's part of the deal. I'm not sure about money. There are laws and things that say we can't be regular employees. Mr. Harlow said he'd work on it with Charlene—she's the one in charge of staff. We'll get whatever meals we want and Wednesdays off. And like I said, we'll probably get some tips, too. Here's the good part: At the end of the summer, just before school starts, we can spend a whole week at the most elegant hotel in Boston, everything free. Your mothers, too. That's the deal. We can start on Saturday if you agree."

Wilma looked at Cathy. "What are you going to do? I think I'd like to try it."

"I have to ask Dad. He'll be back tomorrow night. He travels a lot," Cathy explained to Amy. "He's over in New York State now. Mom says it's all right with her. I'm pretty sure I can do it. Billy's five now. I don't have to look after him."

"Do we still have a club?" Wilma asked.

"Well, we have things to discuss now," Sandy answered. "Let's keep the club."

"We can meet Wednesday evenings," Amy said.

"Here?" Wilma asked. "How about at my house?"

"Here," Cathy said firmly. "This is where we started. We can call ourselves the Graveyard Gang, okay? That will show Bigmouth we won't let him chase us away."

"Okay," Sandy said.

Amy claimed her bike from the shadows. She pushed it along beside Cathy and Wilma, who were chattering about their summer job. Cathy was explaining to Wilma what she should say to her mother. Sandy said good-bye and headed back to Agatha Bates's cottage.

Amy had almost reached the hill to her driveway when a car pulled up beside her. Startled, she slipped off her bike and waited for the car to pass. The car stopped.

"Going home to the palace, are you, Princess?" A familiar voice came from the car. It was Bigmouth, leaning across his silent friend to speak to her. "Be careful on that fancy bike."

Amy didn't answer. She pushed her bike ahead and turned up the driveway. Behind her came the blast of a horn, the blare of rock music, and the spinning of tires on the dirt road.

· 7 ·

It was time to get rid of the old kitchen table with the rusted metal legs and the five chrome chairs with padded plastic seats. Agatha Bates remembered the odd-man-out game— usually the odd-woman-out—at suppertime, which was the only meal, it seemed, the family had managed to take together during vacation. The kitchen table had space for only four chairs. Somehow the boys grabbed the first two chairs, and the third was saved, for no reason Agatha could now recall, for Henry, the father of the family. That left the fourth chair for Agatha or daughter Sarah. The fifth was for the odd-woman-out; Agatha or Sarah had to scrunch at the corner of the table or eat at the counter. Why did I let Henry and the boys get away with that? Agatha asked herself. *I* prepared the meal and Sarah usually helped, while Henry had his gin and tonic on the porch and the boys threw a ball or something.

Well, tomorrow, out the door with the table and chairs. Someone at the town dump, which was open tomorrow, would carry them off, just as Henry, years ago, had brought home from the dump an old oak table and three battered oak chairs. He'd glued the rungs, filled the cracks in the seats, and sanded and oiled the chairs and table to a lustrous patina. Afterward there was no place for them, so they remained in the cellar. When the children had gone for good, Agatha was tempted to throw out the ugly kitchen furniture, but by then the cancer had come and, superstitiously, Agatha feared disturbing the pattern of the past. Henry died with things the way they had always been.

Now these rhythms can be broken, Agatha thought. Sandy and I will bring the oak chairs and table up from the cellar. Would Sandy want to paint them, too? she wondered. It would be a shame, Agatha thought, but perhaps white enamel would complement the yellow cabinets. She wouldn't do it herself—the old superstitions were still strong. She would let Sandy decide.

"What do you think?" Agatha asked after Sandy and she had brought up the oak furniture to the kitchen. "Shall we paint them too—white, I should think—or leave them the way they are?"

Sandy ran her fingers over the surface of the small, round table. How smooth it was. "I don't know, Agatha. It would be brighter, I guess, but I sort of like the wood the way it is."

Agatha watched Sandy take an old towel from the rag-bag drawer and carefully wipe the dust and mildew from Henry's kitchen set. The past had found a future. What a steady, serene child Sandy is, Agatha thought. How fortunate Lydia Prescott was. "The inn is all set?" she asked. "You've passed the papers and everything?"

"Yes, and that job at the Spruce Tree Lodge has come through. At least it has if Cathy's and Wilma's folks will let them go."

"The Graveyard Gang has met, has it?"

"I didn't tell you last night. I had to go talk to Mom first. She and Kate are leaving tomorrow."

"Will the gang need a car pool over to the lodge?" Agatha asked. "I'll join in."

Sandy shook her head. "Nope, they'll pick up and deliver. And at the end of the summer, all of us have a week at the fanciest hotel in Boston. And we'll probably get some tips. It's a good deal for me. I'll learn lots of things about the hotel business."

"I'm sure you will," Agatha said.

"The thing is," Sandy was saying, "just when I have a friend, sort of a friend, anyway, I'll be moving away from that part of town."

"You mean Amy Abbott?"

"Yes. She's not so bad when you get to know her. I mean, she doesn't act like she's so rich. She even tries not to seem rich, can you imagine?"

"She's probably figured out it's more important to have friends than money," Agatha observed. "Did you say she was older than you and the other girls?"

"A year. Something about her father. She missed a year of school, I think, after the accident."

"She was hurt in a car accident?"

"No, it was her father. He was killed when some teenagers didn't stop at an intersection. Amy doesn't talk about it. She wants to, I think, but she can't. That's all she's said."

"I see," Agatha said. "How old was she when it happened, do you know?"

"No. It was four or five years ago, I guess. Her mother has married again, but she's still Mrs. Abbott. She's in the hospital now."

Agatha Bates knew Mrs. Abbott. Rather, she knew *about* Mrs. Abbott. She had been in the general store the day Amy's mother threw one of the famous temper tantrums that the people in Wingate liked to talk about. When Mrs. Reed explained for the third or fourth time that they didn't carry some exotic item, Mrs. Abbott exploded. Almost screaming, she accused Mrs. Reed of running a hick store that sold only canned beans and stale bread, and then stomped out the door to her little sports car. Alice Harper next-door, who kept track of town gossip, reported to Agatha that Mrs. Abbott had also blown up at the library and the post office.

"Amy's mother has caused quite a stir in town, I hear," Agatha said discreetly.

"When the kids talk about Amy, they always end up talking about her mother," Sandy said. "That's not right, is it?"

"No. But that's the way things work sometimes. People in Wingate still find it odd that I am, or I was, a police officer. If you count summers, I'm more of a resident than half the people in town, but that has never made any difference. It's something Amy and her mother will have to put up with when Mrs. Abbott returns."

· 8 ·

"We'll be there, all four of us: Sandy, Cathy, Wilma, and me—I mean *I,*" Amy reported to Charlene Spence.

"Good. We need all the extra help we can get," Charlene told Amy. "A couple of guys we were counting on didn't show up this year. Tell me where to send the driver tomorrow morning. Have your friends be ready at six-thirty. I know it's early, but you can help set up for breakfast."

Amy gave Charlene directions to her house. From there she would direct the driver to the homes of the others. Then she reported back to the Graveyard Gang. To her surprise Wilma didn't complain about the early hour. "That's great," she said. "My mother and I get up with the sun in the summer."

The driver turned the green station wagon around in Amy's driveway. He wore a green Spruce Tree Lodge sweatshirt. "Where do we go from here?"

Amy gave him directions. She sat in back. They could take turns next week if they wanted to. They picked up Cathy, and Sandy, who had walked to Cathy's house; they joined her in back. "Wilma can sit up front," Cathy whispered. "She isn't sure she wants to go. Maybe sitting up front will

27

help." When Wilma opened the back door, Cathy said, "It's your turn to sit in front, Wilma. Tomorrow's my turn." Wilma crept into the front seat and huddled against the door. Amy wondered if Wilma was going to let Cathy tell her what to do the rest of her life.

After the station wagon parked at the rear of the lodge, the driver led them through an enormous kitchen to a room with shelves piled high with linen and china and silver. "Miss Nolan will tell you what to do," he said, pointing to a woman disappearing through a swinging door. "You wait here."

"What a jerk," Cathy said. "He acts like he owns the place."

"Paul said we would have to take it for the first week," Amy replied, "until the staff got used to us. At first they'll think we're dumb kids who will steal their tips."

Wilma stood in the middle of the room looking anxiously around her. "I shouldn't have come. I get frightened in strange situations. What if I drop a plate or do something wrong? My mother said I might have to pay for it."

"No, you won't, Wilma," Amy told her. "They must break things all the time."

"Ah, there you are," said a friendly voice. Miss Nolan came into the supply room through another swinging door. "Charlene said you were a Sandy, a Wilma, a Cathy, and an Amy. Which of you is which? My name is Abby, Abby Nolan. I guess you could call me the housekeeper."

The Graveyard Gang identified themselves. Abby showed them where to find the tableware. "The most important thing to remember here is the swinging doors. Here and in the kitchen, you go out the door on the right, and when you are in the dining room, you come back in through the door on your right. Now, come along with me. I'll give you to Margo.

28

She'll show you what to do. If you have any questions, ask her or one of the waiters."

Margo was a tall, gray-haired woman in a green jacket with a spruce tree on the pocket. "Have any of you set the table at home?" she asked.

Wilma raised her hand halfway.

"You're Wilma, are you? I like the name Wilma. It used to be popular when I was growing up. Okay, Wilma, show me what you can do. There's a tray of silver over by the window."

Wilma returned with a handful of knives, forks, and spoons. She arranged them on the table in front of each chair. "Where are the napkins?" she asked.

"By the door," Margo said. "And bring four soup spoons for hot cereal or whatever. The waiter will take them away if they're not needed. Now, for lunch, a regular fork and a salad fork, and the rest the same. Got that? Also, wipe each piece of silver before you put it down. Makes it shine a little."

Margo looked at her watch. "Seven o'clock. People will start coming in at seven-thirty. Try to be through by then. Then you may have breakfast in the staff dining room. Go in the kitchen and ask. Charlene will pick you up there. Back here at eleven-thirty to set up for lunch. Okay? I'll be around if you have questions."

Breakfast in the staff dining room was put out on a long counter. People hurried in, ate quickly, and hurried away. The girls found a place in the corner to eat. No one even looked at them. A little before eight o'clock, Charlene came over with a cup of coffee to join them.

"I made out worksheets yesterday afternoon," she announced. "They have the jobs you are expected to do, where

29

you are to go, and the name of the person you are to report to. You'll learn the hotel business from the bottom up," Charlene told them. "I wouldn't trade it for any other job in the world. Now, let's see. From here, to help Gus. After that, the room maids. Back here to set up. The rest of the day you will help out—at the pool, on the grounds, in the sun-room and on the terrace, out front at the entrance— wherever anyone needs you. Some of the jobs will probably seem useless to you, but we try to look after the guests in every way we can."

"Mr. Harlow said we shouldn't take tips," Amy said. "What if someone offers us one?"

"Take it, of course. It would be wrong not to. What Bob meant was that if you were helping a waiter or a bellperson, let him or her take the tip. They may share it, or not, I can't say. They are mostly college students who are working their way through. But if you do something by yourself, the money is all yours. Do you understand?"

"Do we shift around in the afternoons?" Sandy asked. "Or stay in one place?"

"You'll probably settle down in one place where you're needed most. But someone else may need you more if they are shorthanded. You'll catch on. I have spoken to the staff heads. They know you are here. Here's a map of the lodge and one of the grounds. I have circled the places where you are supposed to go. Right here, for example, you'll find Gus. He's in charge of grounds. Okay? Good luck. I'm usually in my office off reception if you want me."

The first thing to do, Gus said, was to empty the outside trash baskets and ashtrays. "If you see any trash on the ground, pick it up. That will keep you busy until ten, when you go inside. I'd like one of you in the afternoons to help the grounds keepers. Put the trash in the Dumpster in back of the kitchen."

Amy spread out the map. "Where do you want to go, Sandy?"

"I don't care."

"How about you, Wilma?"

"I don't care, either. I'll go with Cathy and help her."

"It will be better, Wilma, if we divide up the grounds," Sandy said. "Why don't you take the terraces and the tennis courts? I'll go down by the pool and lake. Cathy can do the roadways. That leaves you the rest, Amy. Is that all right with you?"

"Sure," Amy said. "Let's meet here at five to ten. We have to find Martha. She's head of room-cleaning."

Martha assigned one girl to each of the lodge's four floors. "Take the used sheets and towels down to the laundry room for the maids," she instructed. "Empty the wastebaskets in the rooms they are cleaning. It's not much, but it will be a big help to them."

After lunch Cathy headed for the pool. "What about you, Wilma?" Amy asked. "Sandy wants to stay inside."

"I'd like to work out front, unless you want to."

"Fine. I'll go see what Gus wants."

What Gus wanted was someone to collect the grass clippings and carry them to the mulch pile on the other side of the parking lot.

At five they reported to Charlene. "I think that's it for the day," she said. "Some days you'll finish earlier. Charley is outside waiting to take you home. I've already heard how well you've done today. Thanks."

31

·9·

Amy pushed her head from under the covers to look at the wall clock over her bureau. Eight o'clock! She kicked the covers back and scrambled to the edge of the bed. Now she remembered that she hadn't set the alarm on the little travel clock next to her bed. Wednesday! It was Wednesday! Their day off. Through the open window crept a damp mist. Shivering, she pulled it shut. You couldn't see across the valley or to the mountains rising in back of the lodge. It was a good day not to be there.

Wednesday! Tonight the Graveyard Gang had its meeting. Perhaps Sandy would call to say they should skip it this week, and maybe Wilma would want to meet in her house, where she could make popcorn. Cathy would deal with Wilma. Amy determined that *she* wouldn't be the one to back out. They weren't much of a club, only four members, but they had jobs and a place to meet, creepy though it was on gloomy days like today, and they had a weekly meeting time. What more did you do with a club? Amy pulled her knees up to her stomach, turned on her side, and slept.

Once more Amy was the first one to arrive at the cemetery wall. She had left the bike in the garage and walked down the road to Main Street and across to the school yard. By the time she reached the graveyard, her sneakers were soaked. They squished with every step. She stood by the wall, not wanting to sit on the cold, wet rocks. Heavy drops of water fell from the drooping pine branches. The path through the graveyard down to the lake disappeared in the evening gloom. It *was* creepy, Amy decided. Not scary, but creepy.

Cathy and Wilma were wearing plastic raincoats. They were both barefoot. When she saw Amy staring at her feet, Wilma explained that she had only one pair of sneakers, and she had to keep them dry for tomorrow. "I don't like to start the day in wet sneakers."

"You could dry them in the oven," Sandy said.

"I used to, but my mother said they made the kitchen smell bad. Anyway, I go barefoot most of the summer."

Wilma seemed perky to Amy. She was the only one of the three who hadn't uttered a single complaint during their first days at the lodge. Whatever it was she was asked to do, Wilma went at it with good-humored determination. Cathy was the one who fussed a lot, and even Sandy made faces. Once Amy heard her swear under her breath.

"Well, here we are," Sandy said, sitting on the wall. "Sit down, Amy, you can change when you go home. We can't have a meeting standing up."

"What are we supposed to do?" Wilma asked. "Do we elect officers?"

"I don't think we need officers until we have more members," Sandy said. "There's not much for an officer to do, really. Why don't we decide what we're going to do with whatever tips we receive? Do we each keep what we get or should we put them all together for our trip to Boston?"

Amy started to say that she would be given spending

money for the trip. She bit her tongue just in time. "What do you think, Wilma?" She gathered from Sandy that Wilma didn't have much money.

"I don't know," Wilma answered. "I've never had to decide about money before."

"We better decide now," Cathy said. "Dad says money makes more enemies than friends. Is there something you want real bad?"

Wilma shook her head. "My mother's birthday present, that's all."

"When's her birthday?"

"September."

Cathy thought about it for a while. "How about this, then? We'll keep the first five dollars we make each week and put the rest in the club coffee can. I don't know how much we can plan on. Most of the jobs don't pay tips, it seems. Later we can talk about what to do with the club money."

"Agreed." Wilma and Amy said at the same time.

"Who'll keep the money?" Sandy asked.

"Wilma," Amy said. "She can be the club treasurer."

"I'd rather . . ." Wilma began.

"You're outvoted," Cathy said, "three to one. You are the official treasurer, Wilma. We needed an officer for the club, after all. How much did we make? I have three dollars and fifty cents. I helped Roger clean up after a big party in the sun-room. He gave me half. What about you, Sandy?"

"Only a dollar from down at the pool. I kept getting towels for a batch of kids and picking up the wet ones. Their dad gave me a dollar."

"Amy?"

"Nothing. But Gus is teaching me a lot about flowers."

"You, Wilma?"

Wilma turned red. "I'm sorry, but I made a lot. I was waiting to tell you both, but I never had a chance. There was an awful rush at the entrance on Sunday. Everyone was inside when this car came up to be unloaded. The man gave me ten dollars for taking two little bags up to the room."

"That's great, Wilma," Amy said. "Maybe you should keep it all, since you made it before we decided how to divide things up. What do you think, Cathy?"

"Yeah. We'll start dividing tomorrow."

"No," insisted Wilma, "we're a club and we divide equally. That's the way it should be."

A shower of raindrops fell on the girls. The pine branches overhead shook. An object crashed through the branches. It grazed Wilma's shoulder and fell to the ground at her feet. They stared down at it in horror. It was the body of a dead black cat, yellow eyes staring up at them.

Wilma covered her face with her hands. She screamed and ran across the field. Cathy ran after her, calling, "Wait, Wilma, wait for me."

Sandy and Amy, startled, stood up. Through the branches Amy saw Bigmouth climbing down. "I got a mascot for the Graveyard Gang, Princess," he called. He howled with laughter.

Amy sensed a presence at her back. She turned. There on the path, a sick smile on his face, was the ghoul, Perry Whitman. She turned and fled.

35

·10·

"It was Midnight, the Jenkinses' cat," Cathy explained the next morning, as soon as she and Wilma were settled in the back of the station wagon with Amy. "He died of old age, and Mrs. Jenkins told Donald to bury him somewhere."

"Are you okay, Wilma?" Amy asked.

"Today I am. Last night I was scared stiff. I never had a dead cat fall on me before."

"It didn't fall. It was one of Bigmouth's jokes," Cathy said. "Mom was hopping mad when I told her. She went next door right away to speak to Mrs. Jenkins. A lot of good that did. Bigmouth can do no wrong as far as his parents are concerned."

"What are we doing today at the lodge, does anyone know?" Wilma asked.

"The usual, I guess," Amy said. "That's all we've done so far."

Work at the Spruce Tree Lodge settled into a routine. After lunch the regular jobs were finished for the day, and the four girls went in different directions. Wilma, in spite of what she had said about carrying other people's bags, headed for the entrance. She stood to one side until one of the

36

regulars needed assistance. Gradually she was accepted. Ted, the head bellperson, brought her a green shirt. "Join the club," he said. "You can get in line if you want to. Keep your tips. We'll give you a hand with the heavy stuff."

Wilma shook her head. "I can do it by myself," she insisted.

Cathy went down to the pool. In the afternoon they really needed her. She ran back and forth between the pool and the lake, helping guests into the paddleboats and pushing the canoes away from the dock, pumping up bicycle tires, gathering canvas bags of dirty towels to drag up to the laundry room. Other times she baby-sat little kids whose mothers wanted to relax in the sun. Baby-sitting, she discovered, brought in good tips. When she tried to hand the money over to the lifeguard, he told her it belonged to her. He was glad not to have to worry about the kids.

Sandy stayed inside. She made it her job to roam through the big, ramshackle building, half ancient, half very modern, picking up, emptying ashtrays and wastebaskets, straightening chairs in the lounges, and running errands for the guests. All the while she observed how the Spruce Tree Lodge functioned. Her mom would be glad to have the information.

Amy was left to help the grounds keepers, which pleased her more than she expected. It was hard work, the first she had ever done in her life. She felt her body growing stronger. In the afternoons her job involved more than just emptying heavy bags of grass clippings on the mulch pile in the woods beyond the springhouse. She weeded the flower beds, transplanted flowers, and clipped around the putting green. "How are you getting along, Amy?" Mr. Harlow asked about once a week, when he made a survey of the grounds. "I've heard great things about you and your friends. I was pretty smart to take you on, wasn't I?"

"We're getting along fine," she answered. Amy felt good. She wasn't bored. She felt her friendships with Wilma and Cathy and Sandy growing. It was perfect—except for the phone calls!

The third week they were at the lodge, the calls began. The first one came in the middle of the afternoon. Amy was struggling with a plastic bag of clippings when Wilma came running up from the entrance. "Amy, you have a phone call. Milly says it's important. Hurry!"

Amy dropped the bag of clippings, which split open on the driveway. Something must have happened at home. She ran inside to the switchboard. Milly pointed to a phone on the counter. Amy picked it up.

"Hello," she said.

Someone breathed heavily twice and hung up.

"Hello? Hello? Hello?" Amy repeated into the humming mouthpiece.

Perplexed, she turned to Milly. "They hung up."

"Maybe the connection got broken," Milly said. "It happens all the time."

"They asked for me?"

"He sure did, something like, 'Get me Amy. She works there. Tell her it's urgent.' Funny, now that I think about it, just 'Amy,' no last name. You're the only Amy we have. Wait a minute. Maybe he'll call back."

Amy waited. Finally, she told Milly she was going back to work. It must have been a mistake. "But there was someone there. I could hear the breathing before they hung up."

"Oh," Milly exclaimed. "One of those guys? We get their calls here, too. Sometimes they say something dirty in a fake deep voice. Mostly they just breathe. This guy had a fake voice, too, I believe. Sort of slow and heavy. I'll watch for him."

Perplexed, Amy went out to help Wilma, who was picking up the clippings from the road. She was tempted to tell Wilma, but no, she thought. It would just set her to worrying.

The next call came in one morning about a week later, on Milly's day off. Terry was on the switchboard. Amy was on the third floor, vacuuming the hallway. Terry transferred the call to the house phone in the linen closet.

"Hello," Amy said. Once again she heard the heavy breathing. Then the connection was broken. "I'll be right back," she told Martha and ran down to the switchboard.

"It was a man's voice, sort of deep," Terry told her. "He asked for Amy. I asked, 'Amy who?' He said—these are his exact words—'Amy, the one they call the princess.' "

So that's who it was, Bigmouth Donald Jenkins. "Thanks," Amy told Terry. "It's someone playing a joke on me, I think. They hung up when I answered. If the guy calls again when you're on, can you just hang up, please? And tell Milly to hang up, too."

"I will if I recognize him," Terry promised. "Sometimes it might be your folks."

"I know, but they'd tell you who it was."

"Do you know the guy?"

"I think so. It's a teenager in Wingate who's been teasing us."

There were two calls that Milly hung up on, both for Princess Amy, but on the third she had someone fetch Amy from the laundry. "It's for Amy Abbott," she whispered. "It sounds like it might be a woman or a girl. Do you have a sister?"

Amy shook her head. "Hello," she said. And again, "Hello? Hello? Hello? Who is this?" She listened to breathing, steady heavy breathing, then, "Princess?" Amy, frightened now, put down the phone.

"What do I do, Milly? I can't keep him from calling. I'm sorry. Should I quit?"

"Did you talk to your folks?"

"No," Amy said. "Mom's away."

"I think you'd better talk to your father. Terry says you might know who this guy is."

"I think so, but I can't be sure."

"A friend of yours?"

The idea that Bigmouth might be a friend brought a sad smile to Amy's face. "No. We're pretty sure he's a high-school jerk who calls us the Graveyard Gang."

"You talk to your dad," Milly counseled Amy. "Give him Charlene's number to use in case of an emergency. I'll deal with this kook if he calls again."

·11·

As suddenly as they began, the phone calls ceased. Bigmouth no longer kept track of the Graveyard Gang. "Donald has his own car now," Cathy reported. "It's a beat-up old convertible the man at the service station in Coldstream, where he pumps gas, sold him. He doesn't come home until late at night. I don't think he's running around with Perry, either. Mrs. Jenkins told Mom that Bigmouth is talking about learning to be a truck driver. She's afraid he's going to leave home."

"That would be a blessing," Wilma said. "He must have been the one making those calls, don't you think, Amy?"

"I don't know, but I'm glad they've stopped. I'm glad Mom wasn't home. It would have upset her."

"I bet it would," Cathy said. "Everything in Wingate seems to upset her."

"Cathy," Sandy said sharply. "That's none of your business."

"We're friends now, aren't we, Amy?" Cathy persisted.

"I hope so," Amy said.

"Well, what was with your mother? She seemed to think everyone was a hick or her enemy or something. Isn't that so, Wilma? She shouted at your mother in the library, didn't she?"

"That was a long time ago, Cathy. My mother said Mrs. Abbott was upset about something."

Amy had to defend her mother. She wasn't angry with Cathy, but her mom had to be defended. "Mom wasn't feeling well a lot of the time. And she didn't like it here, I admit."

"Why did you move here, then, Amy?" Cathy asked.

"I'm not sure exactly. After my father was killed, she probably wanted to get away. Her painting wasn't working. There were drugs in the schools. Most of all my stepfather wanted to move to the country. He used to stay at the lodge. So they found this place in Wingate. It was a mistake for Mom. Me, too," Amy added. She might as well be honest. "Until this summer. I'm sort of changing my mind. I don't think I want to move back now."

"I'm sorry I asked," Cathy said. "Maybe your mother will change her mind, too, when she comes home."

"Maybe," Amy said, "but I doubt it."

Late in August, on their last day at the lodge, Bob Harlow asked, "Do you think you and your friends can stay a little late tonight? I'd like to invite such a hardworking crew to dinner and see if I can persuade them to return next year."

"Thank you," Amy said, "but we'll have to call our folks."

"I believe Charlene has already done that," Mr. Harlow said. "Why don't we meet in the dining room at seven o'clock?"

Amy looked down at her dirty, grass-stained jeans and worn-out sneakers. "Gee, I don't know. We're not dressed to eat here. People get dressed up to eat in the dining room."

"Just this time doesn't matter," Mr. Harlow said. "Come as you are."

"I'm as sweaty as a pig," Wilma said, when Amy told her. "It must be over a hundred in the shade out there. Sandy's lucky to be inside."

"It's just as hot in the old section. Only the new part is air-conditioned," Sandy said.

"And I'm wet underneath," Cathy said. "I was in a hurry and put my clothes on over my swimsuit."

"Mr. Harlow said we were not to worry," Amy explained. "Come on, we're already late."

Gaston, the *maître d'hôtel,* beamed. *"Bonsoir, mesdemoiselles. Suivez-moi, s'il vous plaît."* He escorted them among the tables to the far corner of the dining room. A flutter of applause followed them across the room. Amy turned red and put her head down. She wondered if Mr. Harlow was playing some sort of joke on them.

Mr. Harlow stood up to greet them. Already at the table were Charley, Gus, Margo, Abby, Ted, the bell captain, and Susan, from the pool. And Wilma's mom, from the library, looking very proud, along with Cathy's mom and dad, whom Amy knew but had never met. And Paul and Stephen. Paul was looking pleased, Stephen bored, as always.

At the end of the meal, Mr. Harlow stood up. "A toast," he said, "a toast to the Graveyard Gang, who did more than anyone else to pull the Spruce Tree Lodge through another summer season. To Amy Abbott, Cathy Cameron, Wilma Hughes, and Sandy Prescott. I think Margo wants to say something."

Margo held some envelopes in her hand. "For the entire staff of the Spruce Tree Lodge, I want to thank the girls for

43

their help. We have all, and I do mean all, chipped in to show our gratitude." She gave each girl an envelope and sat down. Amy peeped. Inside her envelope was a crisp green one-hundred-dollar bill.

Charlene stood up next. She held some more envelopes. "The lodge wants to show its gratitude and pleasure, also." She shook each girl's hand and gave her an envelope. It was Wilma who peeped this time. In happy astonishment she held up two fingers to the others.

"Tomorrow, Charley will drive you down to Boston," Mr. Harlow announced, "for a week in the Parkview. We have told the man in the White House he can't come to Boston next week, because the presidential suite will be occupied by the Graveyard Gang." When the laughter died down, Harlow concluded, "Thank you all for sharing our little celebration. I understand Mrs. Hughes and Mrs. Cameron will be accompanying the Graveyard Gang. We wish you all a bon voyage."

·12·

During dinner, Amy decided not to go to Boston with the gang. I'd be a drag, she told herself, being a know-it-all because I used to live there. Paul had said something about Mom coming home for a weekend, and Stephen was going off to school at the end of next week.

"I don't think I'll go," she confided to Sandy after the banquet. "My mother may be coming home for a couple of days. Tell the others I'm not being snooty or anything. I'd like to go, but I don't think I better."

"You sure?" Sandy asked.

"Yes. Even if Mom doesn't show up, I'd like to be with Paul and Stephen for a while."

Stephen was alone the next morning when Amy came down to breakfast. He was scribbling some figures on a yellow pad. "Where's Paul?" she asked. The study had been empty when she passed by.

"He went to the hospital to see Mom. The doctor called this morning. He said it would be better to wait a while before she comes home for a weekend."

"Oh," Amy said. "Then I guess I could have gone to Boston. How about going to the river with me and Crutch?"

"Can't," Stephen said. "I'm putting an account together

45

for Paul to review before I go off." He nodded and went to Paul's study. She wasn't going to get any company from him, Amy knew. When he was younger, her brother looked after her when things were bad with Mom. Since they moved to Wingate and Stephen had gone off to boarding school, he was a lot different—withdrawn and remote, sort of like Paul. He didn't pay much attention either to Amy or to Mom. Amy sighed. "Come on, Crutch, let's go down to the river."

The old dog limped to the back porch. He stood at the top step and looked down the long path through the meadow. He turned back to the kitchen door and waited to be let inside.

"Too hot for you, Crutch?" Amy asked. "We'll wait until it cools off." She toasted a piece of bread and spread it with strawberry jam. It was going to be a wicked-hot day. She could feel the heat already. I'll go down to the town beach, she thought; maybe there'll be someone there.

Amy slipped into her swimsuit and put on jeans and a T-shirt. "I'm going to the town beach," she called into the study.

There was no response. She called again, louder this time. "I'm going to the beach, Stephen."

"Okay, okay. I heard you," Stephen replied.

In the mornings shade from the tall trees turned old Winthrop Road into a cool tunnel until the sun rose directly above the giant oaks and maples. I'll walk, Amy thought. Then I won't have to worry about my bike.

As she headed toward town she wondered how she was supposed to feel about her mother. Mom was almost like a stranger. Her being gone didn't cause any problem. Amy would get herself off to school like always. Paul would cook supper, the way he had been doing for a while, only maybe he would take turns now with Amy. Mrs. Hubbard would come in twice a week to clean up and do the ironing. Amy had learned a lot during the summer. She knew she could take care of things that might come up while Mom and Stephen were away. "You're a hard worker," Gus had kept telling her. "I could go off on a vacation myself," he had said toward the end of the summer, "and leave you in charge. I wouldn't have to worry." The thought had made her feel good.

Cutting across the soccer field to the graveyard, Amy saw Agatha Bates waving from the side porch. Amy paused. She waved back and turned toward the cottage.

"I'm having a late breakfast," Agatha said. "I was up half the night trying to make my old sewing machine work. You have to use your foot to make it go, can you imagine? Henry bought it at a flea fair for two dollars. We kept papers and magazines on it. Some iced tea? It's going to be a scorcher."

"Yes, thank you. I'm on my way to the pond."

"Your friends are all in Boston for a week, I believe," Agatha said. She wondered why Amy hadn't gone along.

"I couldn't go. Mom was coming home for a couple of days, but she canceled out."

"I see," Agatha said. Sandy had told her Mrs. Abbott had gone off to a hospital. "I hope she'll be all right. If you're lonely at home, come down and help me clean out the cellar. It's cool down there. We can make a start on the yard sale Sandy suggested we have."

"Maybe I will," Amy replied. "I don't think Mom'll be home for a while. She had another breakdown."

"I'm very sorry," Agatha said.

"Mom's had problems for a long time," Amy blurted. "When things get to her, she drinks a lot. Then the depression sets in, and there's nothing we can do. She fades away from us, except the times when she gets angry." Tears came to her eyes. Amy put her hands over her face and sobbed. "And I can't help her. I could never help her. It was like I didn't belong to her or something."

Instinctively Agatha put her arm around Amy's shoulder. She drew the child to her. The only words that came to mind were, "It's all right, child. It will be all right."

Amy slipped from Agatha's arm and buried her face in Agatha's lap. "I want my father," she howled in a breaking voice. "I want my father. I want my father."

·13·

Agatha Bates sat in the porch rocker after Amy had disappeared through the pine trees toward the path down to the lake. Amy had promised to return the next day to help clear out the junk in the cellar. What was going to happen to the child? Agatha sensed she might not be strong enough to withstand the winter loneliness of living in the big white house with a stepfather who apparently had little notion of how to reassure an unhappy fourteen-year-old girl. Sandy would help when she came back, Sandy and the others in the Graveyard Gang. Maybe that would be enough. For the next week, Agatha decided she would try to look after Amy, as much as the girl would allow.

From the fragments of what Amy had told her, Agatha gathered the girl had not completely recovered from the shock of her father's death. Her mother apparently had been in no state of mind to help and had turned Amy over to a therapist and Stephen, her brother. To Agatha's discreet questions, Amy had responded, "I don't remember much about what happened then. There was this woman—I forget her name—I saw a lot. She wanted me to talk, but I don't think I did. Only to Stephen, and he felt worse than I did."

Stephen apparently hadn't needed a psychologist. Unlike

Amy, he had gone to school and dealt with his father's accident in his own way. But Amy hadn't made it to school for a year. She stayed at home with a remote and distraught mother. Agatha had gathered that much from Amy's disjointed confession. Stephen hadn't seen the accident. Only Amy was on the porch looking down the street for her father's car. "He was always on time. Every day at six he would pull into the driveway." Amy clearly remembered an old green convertible with a top that didn't work. Her father had had it since before he and her mother were married. It was the convertible's fault, Amy told Agatha again and again, her anguish fixed on the automobile, not the speeding teenager who smashed into it. It seemed that Amy's dad probably wasn't wearing his seat belt and was knocked from the car to the road. The details were picture-perfect. Agatha guessed they formed a block in Amy's memory to recalling the time before the accident and some of the events after the accident.

I'll do what I can, Agatha told herself. I'm not much of a doctor, but I'm a good listener. She had been the one in the precinct station the other officers wanted in the interrogation room when they sensed a suspect was willing to explain things. "Hey, Agatha," they'd call. "Get in here, and let the guy think you're his mother. He's ready to talk." Sometimes, Agatha remembered, it worked, and sometimes it didn't. More often than not, she would be greeted with a stream of obscenities. But at other times she could sit quietly across the table and listen to the suspect's disturbed outpouring.

Amy knew from last year, when she was new in Wingate, that practically no one in town went to the town beach when

August turned toward September. She had made her way to the lake, or pond, as they called it in Wingate, hoping to find a girl her own age she could introduce herself to and start off the school year with at least one familiar face in the crowd of strangers. It had been as hot last year as it was today, but the beach had been barren. Not even a footprint on the flat, gray sand at the water's edge. Today, it didn't matter; she had friends. Today she wanted to cool off. She made her way through the gravestones to the path that led down a slope to the far end of the pond, away from the beach and parking lot. The pond was pebbly and deep on this end, but kids who really wanted to swim preferred to come here.

Amy slipped out of her jeans and T-shirt. She tiptoed over the pebbles to make a long, flat dive into the dark blue water. She came up shivering. It was freezing. She stroked fiercely to the middle of the pond and turned over on her back. It wasn't so bad out where the sun had been shining. She kicked softly and looked up at the hazy clouds in the sweltering sky.

Should she have told Agatha Bates so much about Mom and herself, things she didn't want the kids to know yet? Things her mother would never forgive her for if they reached the ears of the Wingate women she so despised? Agatha, she was confident, would keep them to herself. She might talk to Sandy, but Sandy was Amy's friend, and she would talk to Sandy herself when she returned to Wingate. She had to be careful this year not to give the kids anything to gossip about. All she wanted was to be one of the gang. No Mercedes, no ten-speed Italian bike, no fancy clothes, no dumb remarks.

"Princess? Is that you, Princess?"

Startled, Amy looked toward the beach. A figure in cutoff jeans dropped from the edge of the big boulder that jutted out from the sand into the water. She heard a loud, "Hi." The figure waved, waded ashore, and jogged toward her. It was Bigmouth Jenkins.

Hurriedly, Amy swam to shore, pulled up her jeans and yanked the wet T-shirt down to her waist. She grabbed her sneakers and ran to the path.

"Hey, wait a minute, Princess." Bigmouth was running now. "Hold on. I'm not going to bite you."

Amy paused. She didn't want Bigmouth chasing after her through the darkening graveyard. Down at the beach, she spied a mother with two kids. Now she wasn't alone. She turned to face Bigmouth. Maybe she'd get up her courage to ask why he'd made those nasty phone calls.

"Where's the rest of the gang?" Bigmouth asked.

"They went to Boston for a week."

"How come you didn't go with them?"

"Because my mother is sick," Amy half-lied.

Bigmouth thought about that for a while. "I'm sorry," he said. "You shouldn't swim here by yourself. Not at this end, anyway. It's real deep out there. If you got a cramp or something, you could drown."

Amy nodded.

"If you want to swim this late, you better go to the beach. I'll be there all week in the afternoon. I quit my job."

Amy nodded again. She felt foolish nodding all the time, but she didn't know what to say. "Next week school begins," she said.

"Yeah, well, I'm not going back this year. I'm seventeen, and the law says I don't have to go anymore."

"Don't your parents make you?"

"They'd like me to go, but it's a waste of time. They understand that. Anyway, I'm thinking of going to a different kind of school. A place they teach you something useful."

I've been here long enough to be polite, Amy told herself. "I have to go home now. It gets dark early."

"Got your bike?"

Amy shook her head.

"I can give you a ride. I have my own wheels now."

"No," Amy replied, terrified. "No, thank you. I have to stop at Mrs. Bates's. I left some things there."

"Okay. Good to see you, Princess. Take care."

·14·

Paul was in the kitchen stirring something that smelled like chili in the heavy yellow pot. "Just in time," he greeted Amy, "to wash your hands and set the table. We might as well eat here in the kitchen for a while. Getting dark earlier, isn't it?"

"I'm sorry," Amy apologized. "I . . ." She was about to say, "I met someone at the beach." Instead, she said, "I stayed at the beach too long, I guess. I had the pond all to myself."

"Is it safe not to have a friend with you? I hear that pond is pretty deep."

"I was all right," Amy said. "I probably won't go in again this year. It was cold."

"Good," Paul said. "Stephen has made the salad. I bought some crusty French bread this morning in Boston. It's great with chili."

When they had taken their places, Paul told them in his cool, calm voice, "I was telling Stephen that we can't expect your mother home for a while. Probably no visits for a month or so."

Amy hadn't figured Mom would be home soon. Stephen

had told her that Mom had been gone for almost six months the first time.

"I won't pretend you and I won't be lonely without Mom and Stephen," Paul said to Amy. "We'll have to do the best we can. There are lots of things we haven't got around to yet. In a month it will be leaf time. We can go up to Mount Lonakee. And we'll pick apples. There are orchards around here where you can pick your own Macintosh and Cortlands. We'll make applesauce and freeze it. There's not much in the freezer now. You can have your friends here for sleepovers on weekends."

"I'll be all right," Amy replied. "The eighth graders will be going on field trips, one of them up to Quebec City. Mrs. Bates and Sandy Prescott and I are having a big yard sale when Sandy gets back. I'm helping Mrs. Bates clear out her cellar."

"That's great," Paul said. "There's a lot of old stuff that was left in the basement here by the people who used to own the house. The workers piled it in a corner beyond the furnace. Why don't we go through it? Perhaps Mrs. Bates would let us add to her stuff."

"I'll ask her," Amy said. Her memory drifted back to the first time Mom went off to the hospital. Had she been gone six months? One day she was home, then she was gone, and after a while she came back. Other thoughts pushed their way into the remembering, the way they always did—the flash of green, the pictures of her father rolling from the convertible to the pavement and lying there without moving while the pickup backed away from the accident and sped down the street, tires squealing as it disappeared around the corner.

She looked up from her plate. The spoon was suspended halfway between her mouth and the plate. Paul and Stephen were staring. "Oh, I'm sorry," Amy stammered. "I was thinking . . . of the old sewing machine Agatha had, the kind you work with your foot. Do you think we have one of those in the cellar?"

"I doubt it," Paul said, "but we'll check it out." Stephen, Amy noted, hadn't stopped staring at her. He knew what she was thinking. Maybe in a day or two, before he went off to school, they could talk the way they used to. The woman doctor had said, "You have to talk it out, Amy. You have to talk about what happened to your dad."

That's what she had done with Agatha, Amy realized. Agatha must have thought she was crazy. She hadn't said much. She had made some sandwiches and lemonade, and they had sat there on the side porch, Agatha's cat purring in her lap while Amy cried and tried to explain how that awful memory swallowed up every other thing she wanted to recall. Afterward Amy had felt refreshed and had gone happily down to the lake and dived deep into the cool water. She hadn't run from Bigmouth. She had talked to him— well, listened, anyway—and answered a couple of his questions. What had he said? That he would be on the beach all week and she should be careful not to get a cramp. She wouldn't be going back to the beach for a while, she told herself.

Or would she? Amy gathered up the plates and silverware. She rinsed them and put them in the dishwasher. She heard Paul say, "We'll turn it on every other day, Amy. There's no point in running it half-empty. I rented some film cassettes in Coldstream. Would you like to watch with Stephen and me?"

"No, thanks," Amy replied. "I walked to Agatha's and back and had a long swim. I think I'll go to bed."

Amy was wearing an old crimson Harvard sweatshirt that must have been her brother's, Agatha thought, or her father's. "Good," she said. "It's chilly down here. And dirty. Maybe I'll go swimming with you this afternoon."

Amy paused before she replied, "It's awfully cold. The pond doesn't get much sun this time of year."

She doesn't want me, Agatha thought. "It's not for me then," she said. "When we first started coming up here in the summer, I used to take the children. There was no beach, no real beach, anyway, just pebbles. I hear they have a proper beach now. Was anyone there?" she asked innocently.

"Only one person," Amy said. "Later, a woman with two kids." She dusted off two large crockery jars. "What are these?" she asked.

"I don't altogether know. They don't look like something Henry would have bought. They were probably here when we bought the place. I wonder if they were for pickling cucumbers or fruit. Look, this one has lovely designs." Agatha pointed to pale blue flowers on the side of the smaller gray crock.

"Dad—Paul, that is—says we have a lot of junk in the cellar that came with our house. Would it be all right if we put any good stuff in with your things?"

"Why not?" Agatha said. "Arthur Harper next-door wants to get rid of a few things, too. We'll sell your stuff and his on commission. What do you think we should charge?"

"You mean we keep part of what we collect?"

"Yes, a certain percentage. What do you say to twenty-five percent, if we haul the things here and clean them up?" Agatha found herself growing excited at the prospect of a giant yard sale. They could start on a Saturday and carry over until Sunday after church was out.

Amy poked around in the piled-up collection of things. "Here's a cradle," she cried. "It's broken at the bottom, but we can fix it, I bet." Amy carefully pulled an ancient wooden cradle to the light from a bulb hanging over the steps.

Henry must have bought the cradle and sneaked it down here while I was working in Boston, Agatha thought. Why, the man was a veritable pack rat. What on earth did her husband think he was going to do with a broken old cradle? Was it to be some sort of sign to his wife that she should give up her job and stay home to produce another child? Agatha felt herself blushing. She would keep the cradle. It looked like a genuine antique. She and the girls could repair it. If she sent it to her daughter Sarah, she might decide to have another baby.

·15·

I'm not going to the town beach, Amy repeated to herself. I'll dive in right here to cool off and go straight home. She piled her shirt and jeans and sneakers out of sight, ran across the pebbles, and plunged into the lake. The water was colder than it had been the day before. Even out in the middle, it was freezing. The sky was cloudy, and the air was turning chill. Amy moved her arms and legs furiously, her head turned away from the beach. If she didn't see Donald Jenkins, she wouldn't have to wave or anything, and she could escape up to the graveyard before he came to where she was. When her toes touched bottom, she shoved her way through the water to the shore.

"Hi, Princess." Lifting her head, Amy saw Bigmouth standing between her and the path. "It's cold today. Come on down to the beach. It's not so deep there. The water is warmer."

"I can't," Amy said. "I just wanted to cool off. I'm in a hurry this afternoon. I'm cooking supper tonight."

"Bring your bike?" Donald asked.

Amy shook her head.

"Okay. Grab your clothes, and I'll take you home."

"I can walk," Amy protested. "I need the exercise."

59

"Nah. It's still too hot to walk. Come on. I'll have you home in ten minutes." Bigmouth strode ahead, Amy meekly following, carrying her clothes.

"There!" Bigmouth pointed to a dirty black automobile in the beach parking lot. "How about that for a car?"

"Gosh." Amy tried to admire the old car. "What is it?"

"A Pontiac. It needs some work. A new muffler, hubcaps, maybe a coat of paint. I haven't decided yet. Get in." Donald swung the door open and bowed.

Amy put on her jeans and shirt and rubbed the sand off her feet and jammed them into her sneakers. She guessed it was all right to ride with Bigmouth. He wasn't altogether a stranger, and he *did* live next door to Cathy. She eased herself into the passenger seat, which collapsed beneath her weight.

"Real leather seats, too," Bigmouth said. "The springs are a little soft. Here, I'll get rid of these." He pulled an overflowing ashtray from the dash and emptied it to the ground. "I can't smoke at home. Dad has lung trouble."

Amy sank back in the seat, hoping she would be out of sight as they went down Main Street. "It's nice," she said. "Where did you get it?"

"From a guy at work. I pumped gas all summer at Sam's Sunoco station in Coldstream. Sam got it from his brother-in-law. Only seventy thousand miles on it. Dad says it was a steal. He used to work on cars." Bigmouth found a station that was playing hard rock. When he turned the ignition, the Pontiac rattled and shook, before it settled down to a steady roar. "It's only the muffler," Donald explained. "We'll take care of it tomorrow."

Amy braced herself for the car to accelerate in a shower

60

of gravel. Instead, Bigmouth made a wide, slow turn out to the road. "It's better not to push it, Sam said, until it's ready. Then, watch out!"

I can't call him Bigmouth, Amy thought. So far she had avoided using any name at all. I don't want him to call me Princess. "My name is Amy," she said softly.

"I know it is, but I like to call you Princess. You're the only one we have in this hick town. You can call me Donald. I'm getting too old to be called Bigmouth."

They came to Main Street. Amy saw some kids outside the general store and slid deeper into her seat, only the top of her head rising above the door. "It's really comfortable," she told Donald.

"Yeah, I know. I took Mom out for a ride. She said it made her feel like a teenager again."

Donald headed up Old Winthrop Road. "They ought to pave this road," he complained. "Maybe your father could get them to do it. He's pretty important, they say. They sure enough aren't going to pave it for the Prescotts and Whitmans."

They passed the rutted dirt road to the Whitmans' run-down farm. Amy was sitting up now. "Did Perry Whitman work with you this summer?" she asked politely.

"No, I reckon he helped his dad on the farm. I haven't seen him for a while."

That was interesting. Amy figured the ghoul was the first person Donald would have shown his new car. They were coming to the Prescotts' mobile home on the left. "That's where my friend Sandy Prescott lives. Used to, I should say. They're going to move."

"They are?" Donald asked. "When I first had my driving

61

permit I drove Dad's car down their road a couple of times late at night. I'd turn around at the end and race back blowing my horn."

"Why did you do that?"

"I don't know. Something to do. Blowing your horn at night is a big deal in Wingate. Where are the Prescotts going?"

"They bought the old inn on lake something or other."

"Lake Matusset?"

"That's it. Is there a beach there?" Amy asked.

"Just at the inn. It's too far from the center to be the town beach. There's a boat landing, if you have a speedboat. Well, here we are." Bigmouth pulled into Amy's driveway. He looked at his watch. "Eleven minutes, just like I said. I can do it in five. But Chief Torbert would tell my folks."

Amy threw open the door and had her feet on the ground before Donald stopped the car. "Thanks a lot," she said, slamming the door.

"Hey, wait, Princess. I'll drive you up."

"There's no place to turn around if both cars are outside," Amy lied.

"Ashamed of me, or my old car?" Bigmouth asked.

Amy shook her head. "It's just that . . ."

"It's okay. Your mother thinks the people in Wingate are dirt. That's okay with me. I don't think much of some of them, either."

"It's not that," Amy began.

"It's okay, I said. No big deal. Don't worry about it. See you tomorrow, rain or shine?"

"Maybe," Amy replied. She smiled and headed up the driveway.

·16·

By noon on Friday Agatha and Amy had sorted out the stuff in the cellar for the mammoth yard sale to be held on the front lawn the first or second weekend in October, depending on whether the fall leaves turned early or late. "We'll see how it goes," Agatha said to Amy. "The swamp maples have already begun, but that doesn't mean anything, they say. Do you have much stuff to add?"

Amy had forgotten about the things in their basement. She wouldn't be going to the beach on Saturday and Sunday; she and Paul would be getting Stephen off to school. She could check out the basement then. She helped Agatha spread a couple of old sheets over pieces of furniture and crockery and toys that were to be kept. None of them seemed very precious. They were more like memories for Agatha. "Why, this old sled is worthless!" she had exclaimed when they came to a runner sled with rusted runners and a broken board. "Henry was going to fix it up for one of the boys, I remember. You and Sandy and I can do something about it this fall, and I'll send it off to John. He lives outside New Haven. They'll have some snow there."

Now Amy had to hurry down to the beach. She had promised to bring sandwiches and a couple of apples. She and

63

Donald had agreed to have a picnic on the boulder. Amy had not dared to make the sandwiches at home. Stephen would ask her something nasty in his preppy accent, or Paul would offer to help. He wouldn't ask any question but you could tell he would be curious. Amy didn't want to have to lie, like saying they were for Agatha and her.

Agatha wouldn't ask, she was sure. She might not even pay attention. Mostly Agatha listened to her, Amy realized. She was that way with Sandy, too. Agatha respected the girls' privacy. In the kitchen, Amy called, "Could I take a couple of sandwiches to the beach, Agatha, and an apple or two?"

"Of course, help yourself. There's some cream-cheese spread in the refrigerator and the usual peanut butter and jelly—apple, I think. It's the old-fashioned peanut butter. I bought it by mistake. You have to mix the oil into the peanuts. Holler if you want something."

Agatha sat down on the old sofa she meant to replace. Should she sell it or not? she pondered. It was a good piece, but it needed to be upholstered, and she suspected some of the springs were loose. She shivered. In Wingate you never turned the furnace on until October; it was some sort of tribal law. Her thoughts drifted to Amy. What on earth was the child making a picnic lunch for on this chill, damp day? And *who,* or whom, was she making a lunch for?

Yesterday and Wednesday, also, both wretched, gray days, Amy had excused herself in the middle of the afternoon. Agatha, looking out the kitchen window, not spying, mind you, only looking, watched Amy weave her way through the pine trees and grave markers. She was walking fast, giving a little skip every so often. She was going to meet someone. That was certain. Equally certain, Agatha was convinced, it was a boy.

Amy was a year older than Sandy, Agatha knew. In many ways she was far less mature than Sandy, but if you put the two of them side by side, you'd see the difference right away. Not physically different—who could tell these days how old a girl teenager was in her jeans and baggy shirts? No, it was that Amy understood somehow that she was a year older than the others and let them know it.

A boy? How silly. Amy probably had found a girl from school at the beach, a lonely kid like herself. A lonely kid, maybe, but a boy? No, it must be a girl. Amy hadn't said anything to Agatha because she didn't want to be disloyal to her Graveyard Gang, her first and up to now only friends in Wingate. That was it. No, it wasn't. Amy Abbott was skipping through the graveyard to meet a boy. *That* was it. "Good-bye, Agatha," she had called when she was outside, and stuck her head inside to tell Agatha she'd be by after school next Tuesday. Out there she was safe from questions. It was a boy. But who?

"I made four sandwiches," Amy said to Donald, "two cream cheese with chives and two peanut-butter-and-jelly. They might be runny. I didn't mix the oil in. And two apples. Macs, I think."

Bigmouth held up the apple, turning it around to take a close look. "Nah, it's a Cortland. I like them better, anyway. Mom always gets Cortlands."

Amy smiled. She had discovered that Donald wasn't always easy to please. He had let her know that he was an expert on New Hampshire, particularly Wingate, like when he told her he went deer hunting with his dad. Amy had looked at him in horror. "Sure," he had said, laughing. "That's what they're out there for, to be shot and frozen. Venison is real good."

"But . . ." Amy had begun.

"Deers aren't Bambis, Princess," he told her. "They eat up your garden. The year before you moved in, Dad killed a big buck right there in the pasture in back of your house."

That was how you grew up in Wingate, Amy supposed. Mom had seen it right away and she hadn't liked it. Some things I'll have to get used to, Amy thought.

It was the other side of Donald Jenkins that Amy was attracted to, the lonely, sometimes angry side she would never have imagined was there. Bigmouth—Donald would always be Bigmouth to her—wasn't a stupid boy. He couldn't express himself too well, but he had things to say that Amy could understand.

"Don't think I'm a dumb hick, Princess. Don't you think I'm dumb because I stayed back in school," he told her Thursday while they sat on the boulder watching a soft rain splatter the surface of the pond. The drops had collected on his thick brush of hair and trickled over his bushy eyebrows. Donald's eyes were dark and set deep in his face.

"I don't think that," Amy defended herself. "I stayed back a year."

"You did? You? I don't believe that. How come you stayed back? Girls never get held back. Teachers have it in for boys, specially the old-women teachers. What was *your* problem, Princess?"

"My dad died, and I couldn't pay attention in school. I kept thinking of him and not my schoolwork. They told my mom it would be better if I stayed back a year."

Donald was upset, she could see. It was something beyond

his Wingate experience. He shook his head, as if he hadn't heard it right. "Gosh. That's too bad. Your mom's sick, too, now? What's she got?"

Amy shrugged. "She'll be all right soon," she told Bigmouth. "Some sort of virus."

"In school I couldn't sit still," Bigmouth went on. "And I didn't do my work. Most of all, I talked back to the teachers. Sometimes they sent me home."

"What did your parents say?"

"They took my side," Bigmouth answered. He paused. "I reckon they shouldn't have done. It made me cut up more."

"Did you have any friends?" Amy had asked when Donald tried to explain his loneliness, how he was all by himself inside.

"Only Perry Whitman, and everyone says he's crazy. No matter, he's smart. He didn't start school until he was eight."

"How come?"

"The school people didn't know he was there." Donald hooted. "Can you beat that? He lived right there on the edge of town with his father, who's gone in the head, and no one knew about him. It turned out he was a genius, they say. He used to help me with my homework." Donald sighed. "He was the only friend I had. He did something real dumb this summer that made me mad. I haven't seen much of him since."

Amy didn't ask what it was. Bigmouth would tell her if he wanted to. It began to rain hard. "We better go," Amy said.

"It's just rain."

"We better go. They'll want to know why I'm soaked."

"Okay. If you say so, Princess. I put the top up this morning. New muffler, too. See you tomorrow?" Bigmouth asked.

"I can't. We have to get my brother ready for school."

"Sunday?"

Amy shook her head.

"One last swim?" Donald was pleading now.

Amy was thinking: Monday, Stephen would be gone. If it was like the last three days, no one would be at the beach. "Okay, Monday afternoon, late. If I'm not here by four-thirty, I'm not coming."

"No buts, Princess. Just promise to come." He held out his hand. "Promise?"

Amy took his hand and shook. "Promise."

·17·

Amy sat in the back of the Mercedes looking out the window. In front Stephen was earnestly telling Paul about the Sherburn account. Paul had to pay special attention to it; it looked to Stephen as if they were overloaded in real estate, and Mr. Sherburn wouldn't listen to Stephen, something like that. Paul said he'd take care of it on Monday, that Mr. Sherburn was sometimes too conservative for his own good.

Amy smiled to herself. Donald was just about as old as Stephen. She tried to imagine her brother sitting on the boulder at the town beach telling her about his old car. Or wearing a torn black T-shirt advertising Sam's Service Station in Coldstream, New Hampshire. Stephen didn't have to worry yet about shaving. Bigmouth had been shaving for over a year, he had told Amy. He had lifted her hand to feel the black stubble on his cheek. Amy giggled.

Never missing what was going on around him, Paul glanced over his shoulder. "Yes, Amy?"

Amy shook her head. "Nothing, I was just talking to myself."

"I'm sorry," Paul apologized. "I was giving all my attention to Stephen's problem."

"It's okay," Amy responded. She thought about Dunning,

the school Stephen attended. Dunning was the same school Dad had gone to. Maybe that was why Stephen hadn't started off there. Mom hadn't exactly said no when Paul had suggested Dunning three years ago. She only said she wanted her children at home, but Stephen told Amy it was because she wanted to feel she had some control over her kids. Even though Dad was gone, she still wasn't going to let anyone influence decisions about Stephen and Amy. "It's some kind of guilt feeling, I guess, for not paying attention to us the rest of the time." Stephen was big on guilt feelings.

But guilt hadn't kept Mom from yanking Stephen out of the regional high school at Christmas last year when she found out the boy sitting next to him on the bus had an Elvis Presley tattoo on his arm, and that half the boys wore boots and biker jackets. And one of the boys, Amy suddenly recalled, was called Bigmouth and had teased Stephen about his preppy clothes. Some of the boys and girls snuggled in the back of the bus. Stephen was packed off to Dunning as soon as Paul persuaded the headmaster that, because Stephen was the son of the late Harry Abbott, he absolutely had to be let in at midyear.

"Hey, Stephen," Amy spoke up. "Do you remember a guy named Bigmouth who dropped a dead cat on us at the graveyard? Didn't he use to tease you on the bus last year?"

"Yeah, at first," her brother admitted. "What about him?" Stephen's calm, flat voice was more and more like Paul's.

"Nothing. I just wondered."

"What made you think of him?" Stephen asked. "I'd forgotten all about Bigmouth. He was all right after the first couple of weeks. He sat next to me sometimes. He hated school. Is he still around?"

"I think so," Amy replied. "Cathy says he might go off

to be a truck driver." Another lie. What made her want to talk about Donald Jenkins? Amy shivered. I can't keep on lying, she told herself. I've lied to Agatha—not directly, but still I lied—and sort of to Paul, to Donald, and now to Stephen. The lies were going to catch up with her. She hoped Donald would go off to truck-driving school, the way he said he would. Talking to him at the beach was all right, she supposed. She couldn't be rude to Bigmouth. And talking to him made her feel grown-up in ways she could only admit to herself. She bet that Cathy, who lived next door to him, didn't know him as well as she did. Still . . .

Amy knew what Cathy and Wilma would say if they found out she and Bigmouth shared a picnic at the beach. Thank heavens no one had been there. No one had come to the beach the whole week except for the woman with the little kids last Monday, and she hadn't paid any attention to the two people at the other end of the pond. If Amy kept on, however, it wouldn't take long for the girls in the eighth grade to find out. They'd giggle and whisper and pass notes behind her back. Sooner or later Mom would find out when she came home; the idea of her daughter riding around in a convertible with Bigmouth Jenkins would put her back in the hospital in no time at all.

Tomorrow she would tell Donald she wasn't coming to the beach anymore this year and that she had to go straight home after school to do her homework and help out in the house. No rides, thank you. I need the exercise I get walking to school and back. Amy settled back in the soft, leather seat. I have to do it, she told herself. No matter how I really feel, no matter what Bigmouth says, I've got to do it. All the while a little voice inside her head kept saying, I don't want to.

71

Monday was yet another cold, damp afternoon. Amy carried a nylon jacket Mom had bought her and Amy had never used. Bigmouth had on a black leather jacket over the T-shirt and cutoff jeans he wore to swim in. He was standing at the water's edge, digging his toes into the sand. "There might be a frost tomorrow night, Princess, Dad said. Up on the hill you probably won't get any."

Amy nodded.

"Dad and I have the heater working in the convertible. It was only a loose wire."

"That's good. You'll need it this winter."

"I dunno. Not too much, maybe. The best truck-driving schools are down south, Sam says, in North Carolina and Georgia. It don't, doesn't, I mean, get so cold down there, does it?"

"I don't think so." Was Bigmouth trying to use better English because of her? "Are you going off, then?" she asked.

"I just might. My folks won't think much of it. That's for sure. Will you miss me, Princess?"

Amy did not answer at once. At last she made herself say, "I guess so. If you don't, will you go back to school?"

"Nah, I won't ever do that. I might go back to Sam's. He said he'd start me in the repair shop. I'd make a lot more than I do pumping gas and cleaning windshields. What do you think?"

"I don't know." She had to leave. The conversation was something she hadn't counted on. "I have to go in a minute. Paul needs me to clean the house."

"I thought Mrs. Henday came in to clean and do your housework. My mom knows her."

"She can't come tomorrow." Another lie. What if Mrs.

Jenkins found out? Something else came to mind. What had Donald told his parents about her? Donald hadn't said anything, but it sounded as if he discussed everything with his folks. She couldn't ask now. Right now she wanted to run, to slide off the rock and scoot down along the edge of the lake to the path and escape to Agatha's. "I have to go, Donald, really." She jumped to the beach.

"Okay. I'll get you back fast today." Before Amy could move, Bigmouth took her arm and led her to the car lot.

"It takes a while for the heater to warm up," Donald said. He threw his jacket into the back. "Can you feel it coming out?"

"Yes. It doesn't matter." She twisted the jacket in her hands. "Could we go now?"

"What's the matter, Princess? You're scared of me again, aren't you? I told you I wasn't going to bite you. We'll leave in a second." Bigmouth turned to face Amy. "All I want to know is whether you'll miss me if I do go down south. Would you be my girl while I'm gone?"

Donald's arm moved around Amy's shoulder. It drew her closer to his face. He pressed his mouth close to hers. Amy jerked her face away. She threw open the door. As she ran past the front of the Pontiac to the lake, she heard Donald call, "Hey, wait a minute, Princess, I'm sorry. Come back, Princess."

73

·18·

"Do you want a ride to school?" Paul asked.

"No, thanks. Only when it rains," Amy replied. She dropped an apple on top of her lunch in its paper bag. She folded the bag neatly at the top and put it in an old canvas bag, along with last year's Trapper Keeper notebook. Old things were the things to have at the Bromfield Elementary School, canvas bags with advertising on the side and old three-ring notebooks from your brother or sister—and paper lunch bags, absolutely.

"I'll be back about five, before it gets dark," she promised Paul. "I might go out for the soccer team. This year it's a boys-and-girls team."

"Take care," Paul said. He followed her to the door. "Anything special for supper?"

Amy shook her head. "It's my night to cook, isn't it?"

"Yes, but it's also the first day of school."

"No," Amy said firmly. "We divided the jobs up. I missed a day last week. I'll do it. See you at five."

As she started down the driveway, a terrifying thought came to her. What if Bigmouth was waiting for her? She could just see herself in the front seat of the dented old Pontiac driving up to the school. She slowed her pace. She

74

peered beyond the curve. Old Winthrop Road was clear. Unless he was parked at the top of Perry Whitman's lane, Donald wasn't going to bother her.

Amy had shoved yesterday's episode out of her mind. Bigmouth hadn't meant her any harm. He was going off, and that was his way of saying good-bye. She shouldn't have been startled and run off. She should have stayed and told Donald something that would have made him take his arm away. She wasn't sure what—something like, "Please don't" or something. She wondered if Donald was one of those boys who Stephen had said snuggled with girls in the backseats of the regional high-school bus.

It had rained hard during the night. The water was still dripping off the roadside trees, and Amy moved to the middle. There were big puddles you had to avoid. Amy glanced at the Prescott place. No sign that Sandy's mother had brought her back. When she came to the Whitmans', she saw that the lane was empty. At Main Street Amy walked faster. Ahead, in the middle of the sidewalk, Cathy and Wilma were waiting. Amy began to run.

The two girls hugged her. "It was awesome, Amy!" Wilma exclaimed. "Really awesome. We had the whole top floor of the hotel, it seemed like. Didn't we, Cathy? What did they call it?"

"The penthouse. We had most of it, I guess." Cathy agreed. "There were rooms we didn't use, except when Sandy's mother and Kate came to spend the night."

"Every morning they'd wheel these carts into our private dining room with our breakfast," Wilma interrupted. "You called the night before and put in your order from this big menu. Anything, absolutely anything you wanted. The waiter said the president of the United States and his wife spent two days there last year. Imagine, the president of the United States. My mother said she'll be talking about it the rest of her life. She voted for *him,* you know, Cathy. Your folks voted for the other man."

Cathy paid no attention. "We're sorry you couldn't come. What did you do? How's your mother?"

Amy hesitated. She couldn't lie to the Graveyard Gang. They had been together too long. "Not too good." It was easier to talk about Mom than Bigmouth. "She didn't come home. But she'll be all right soon."

The first bell rang. Cathy and Wilma reached out to take Amy by the hand. "The three musketeers," Wilma sang. "Together through thick and thin, we're the Graveyard Gang. That doesn't rhyme, does it? Anyway, that's our club song."

"Sandy's coming up from Boston tomorrow," Cathy said. "She doesn't want to get too far behind with the new teacher. She's Miss Wilder, Ms. Wilder, maybe. She's Canadian, Mom says."

The new teacher was a tall, friendly looking woman, not too old, Amy decided, about thirty. "I'm Helen Wilder," she told the class when the shuffling and whispering had stopped. "I'm from Toronto, Canada. Who knows where that is?"

Five or six hands went up tentatively.

"Well, by the end of the year, the rest of you will know," Miss Wilder went on. "And some of you will wish you had never heard of it—or of me, either."

The class laughed nervously.

"I have only two rules: no talking in class and homework always done on time. No excuses."

A sigh of relief passed through the classroom.

At lunchtime the gang took their paper bags to the grave-yard wall. Wilma opened her bag and sniffed. "Peanut butter and jelly like always. Don't you wish we were at the Spruce Tree Lodge? The lunches were super. You should have seen the dining room at the Hotel Parkview where we ate supper. There goes the bell."

Amy glanced at her watch. Miss Wilder was saying something in French to see who in the class understood. One-thirty, another hour of school. No homework tonight, Miss Wilder had said, but starting tomorrow, homework every night, even over the weekends. From the corner of her eyes, Amy saw the town cruiser pull into the school driveway. It stopped, and Chief Torbert got out and headed for the principal's office. About ten minutes later he climbed back into the cruiser and drove away.

Five minutes after that, Mr. LaGrange, the principal, came into the room. He whispered briefly to Miss Wilder and left.

"There's a school meeting now in the auditorium," Miss Wilder announced. "Classes are dismissed after the meeting." She held the door open while the class filed out.

Mr. LaGrange stood on the stage with a couple of the older teachers. When Miss Wilder pulled the double doors shut at the back of the auditorium, the principal spoke. "I am very sorry to have to announce that a former student of the Bromfield School has had a fatal accident. Donald Jenkins was drowned last night at the town beach. Please rise and bow your head in silent prayer for Donald."

Amy stumbled to her feet, her heart beating wildly. She lowered her head. What had happened? Something was wrong. It couldn't have been Donald. He was a super swimmer. Her thoughts became confused. Maybe it wasn't really

Donald. What was Bigmouth doing at the beach last night? Why did he go into the water? It was bitter cold, too cold to swim, Donald had told her. Why? It made no sense. Why? Why? Why?

The kids filed quietly from the auditorium. As she passed outside, a thought jolted Amy. Bigmouth had killed himself because of her. No, she moaned and ran down Main Street and the road home.

·19·

Paul was in his study, half a sandwich and a cup of coffee on the computer table. He turned his chair toward the door as Amy tiptoed by. She saw him glance at his watch before he spoke. "You're home early," he said. "Is something the matter?"

"We got out early," Amy replied. "I wasn't feeling too hot, anyway. I'm going to lie down."

"Why didn't you call? I'm always here, Amy."

"I forgot to take a dime. I thought I'd walk it off. I'm probably just tired."

Amy huddled in her bed, knees drawn up almost to her chin. Outside, the sun had at last appeared. The maples along the driveway were touched with red and yellow. Fall was going to be early after all. She thought back to Tuesday last week. It must have been about this time, maybe a little later, when she went to see Donald's new car. She pushed the memory away and closed her eyes.

There was a tap on the door. Then it opened. Amy pretended sleep. Without a word, Paul put something on her bedside table. The door clicked shut. Amy didn't look. It had to be ginger ale and saltines. That was what Paul always brought her when she had a cold and had to stay in bed.

What was she supposed to feel about Bigmouth? All the way home she had refused to let herself think about him. Not until she was safe in her room had she opened her mind to what Mr. LaGrange had announced, that Donald Jenkins, a former student at Bromfield, had drowned. Amy visualized Bigmouth stepping out of his car and walking slowly but purposefully to the beach, scuffing his feet in the sand the way he did, and not stopping at all but walking straight into the pond beside the boulder until he came to the deep part and the water closed over him.

A scream took shape. Her mouth opened as the sound came pushing out. Amy jammed her forearm between her teeth and bit hard. The scream turned into a hollow sob. No, no, no, that wasn't what happened. People like the bearded, half-tough Bigmouth Jenkins didn't kill themselves. Or, if they did, Amy was pretty certain, they used a gun, the gun they shot deer with, or they drove their car into a tree or a light pole as fast as they could.

Donald hadn't taken his own life over a little thing like Amy's refusing to kiss him. What had he shouted after her? Something like, "Hey, Princess, come back," or, "Wait a minute, I'm sorry." If there was anything else, Amy hadn't heard it. She was beyond the beach splashing her way across the wet pebbles toward the graveyard path.

What Donald had done, she convinced herself, was to sit behind the wheel of the Pontiac for a while, fiddling with the knobs on the radio, then with the key chain, making up his mind for good to go to the truck-driving school. He decided to take one last swim before he left Wingate. She saw him push open the car door, climb to the outside of the boulder, stand there for a moment in his cutoff jeans and

80

T-shirt before he plunged into the ice water. A cramp had seized him. That was what had happened. Hadn't he warned her two or three times about getting a cramp in the pond?

Reassured, Amy turned on her back. She stared at the ceiling, where the sunshine formed strange patterns. For a moment Amy felt relief. Now she wouldn't have to worry about Bigmouth Jenkins. She could go back to her friends. Instantly relief was followed by guilt. It was her fault. She had left Donald there by himself, and whatever had happened was partly her fault. He had warned her about getting a cramp, but she hadn't given him a thought, she was so frightened. And what was so wrong with a kiss, only one, to tell Donald good-bye? He was her friend. They had talked and shared lonely secrets. She had told him about herself and about her father's accident. There wasn't anything wrong with Bigmouth. It was wrong for her to worry what the kids or her mother would say if she rode in his convertible. Cathy and Stephen both said he was all right. Paul wouldn't have done anything; he might have told her to ask Donald to come to supper. That's the way Paul was. He could have come on Amy's night to cook. She saw him at the kitchen table, fiddling with his knife and fork. Now Amy cried. Sobbing, she fell asleep.

"Amy," a quiet voice filtered into her slumber. "Amy, your friend Cathy is on the phone. Shall I tell her to call back?"

Abruptly, Amy sat up. It was almost dark outside. The room was dim, and she could smell the heat from the radiator in the cold room.

"Hello, Cathy," she whispered. She heard the click as Paul hung up the phone downstairs.

"Are you all right, Amy?" Cathy demanded. "I wanted to call. Why did you run away? You were as white as a ghost."

"I didn't feel well. I was upset at what happened. I remembered the dead cat and things like that. They upset me."

"Me, too," Cathy agreed. "Bigmouth lived right next door, you know. We were sort of friends. It's awful what happened."

"Yes," Amy said.

"The Jenkinses have collapsed. Mom was next door for a while. Bigmouth was all they had. Mr. Jenkins isn't all that well, anyway. He was a heavy smoker and has something in his lungs. Empha—something or other."

"Emphysema."

"Yeah, that's it. He wouldn't let Donald smoke, but he did, anyway."

"I know," Amy confessed.

"You do? How do you know?"

Amy thought fast. "He was smoking a cigarette the night he blew his horn at Sandy and me for walking on the wrong side of the road."

"Oh. Mom says Chief Torbert thinks he hit his head diving from the rock. She can't figure out what he was doing at the pond this time of year. In the rain, too."

Amy didn't answer. She didn't trust herself to say anything about the accident.

"Are you there, Amy? What's wrong?"

"Nothing. I'm just dopey. I was asleep. I think I'm getting a cold."

"You don't sound so good," Cathy said. "You ought to stay in bed for a day or two. Sandy comes home tomorrow, did you hear?"

"Wilma told me."

"She'll be in school Thursday. Isn't that great? When will we have a meeting of the Graveyard Gang?"

"I don't know. Whenever you want."

"Wilma says the club has some money left over. We have to decide what to do with it. Maybe we should send some flowers to Donald's parents."

"That's a good idea," Amy said. "Tell Wilma to go ahead. I have to go back to bed now, Cathy. I'll call tomorrow if I don't make it to school."

"Take care, Amy. See you Thursday or Friday."

Amy put down the phone. Puzzled, she sat in Stephen's desk chair. Donald didn't hit his head. Chief Torbert was wrong. It was a cramp. The hole at the diving end was really deep. Donald dove in Wednesday, or was it Thursday, and went down to the bottom. He came up breathless. "It's really deep," he sputtered. "Twenty feet or so, I bet." Donald hadn't hit his head, Amy was certain. It was a cramp. Bigmouth had gone down to the bottom again yesterday and caught a cramp.

· 20 ·

Agatha Bates pulled open the front door, then the side door, to let the sun-warmed breeze pass through the living room. Both doors were swollen tight in the humidity, which had also brought out of the walls every ancient smell the house had collected in one hundred and fifty years: old plaster smells, farm smells, cooking smells, all mixed in with other, more subtle odors Agatha could not recognize. Why didn't I turn on the furnace during the rainy spell? she asked herself. Am I so bound into New Hampshire traditions that I can't take charge of my own house? The next cold snap, no matter what the calendar said, she would turn it up to sixty-five degrees, no, all the way up to seventy degrees, and dry out the house. She stepped out to the porch. The sunshine slanted across the soccer field, which soon would be filled with young teenagers. This year, Sandy had told her, the school team would be boys and girls both—only, it seemed, because there weren't any worthwhile boy soccer players in the eighth grade.

Agatha noticed a crowd of children passing quietly out the school's side door. No shouting and running and pushing. Others made their way to the sidewalk along Main Street from the front door. Agatha saw a familiar figure dart ahead of the rest. It looked very much like Amy Abbott. Agatha glanced at her watch; it was hardly one-thirty. Did school let out early the first day of classes?

Amy seemed to be in a hurry to get home. She had half-promised on Friday to come by this afternoon after school. Yesterday afternoon Agatha had seen Amy, or someone who resembled Amy, jump over the graveyard wall and cut across the soccer field toward Old Winthrop Road. She must have gone swimming again, though Agatha couldn't imagine anyone at the lake on such a dismal afternoon.

The Tebbetts boy waved as he ran between Agatha's and the Harpers' house. This year he was wearing a Pirates, not a Red Sox, cap. "They let you out early, did they, Billy?" Agatha called.

Billy came over to the porch. "Didn't you hear? One of the boys who used to go to our school was drowned at the pond, Bigmouth Jenkins. He used to tease me, called me Billy Two-Bits."

"I hadn't heard," Agatha said. "When did this happen?"

"Mr. LaGrange said last night. I guess they didn't find him until today. Otherwise, we wouldn't have had any school at all. See you, Mrs. Bates." Billy took off at a run, in case his mother hadn't heard about Bigmouth Jenkins.

Agatha frowned and pursed her lips. Donald Jenkins was slightly more to her than a stranger. She recalled he had been a problem for the Graveyard Gang early in the summer. Sandy had mentioned once or twice that the Jenkins boy might be making anonymous phone calls to Amy at the lodge.

Could it have been Bigmouth that Amy was making sandwiches for? What a ridiculous notion, Agatha told herself. You're not a cop any longer. You're a widow living in a small

85

New England town where Chief Torbert and his deputy play checkers most of the time, because they don't have anything to do. But why was Amy running like crazy away from her friends the moment school let out? Disasters like drowning and fatal car accidents didn't happen in Wingate all that often. They took a lot of talking about when they occurred. But Amy hadn't lingered to talk to the gang, she'd headed for home. What about yesterday? What was she doing rushing up from the pond late yesterday afternoon without a glance at Agatha's house? Probably to cook supper. She and her stepfather were taking turns, she had told Agatha. I am being silly, Agatha recognized. That was what happened when you lived by yourself, you made up little dramas to get you through the day.

But Agatha knew she wouldn't rest easy until she found out what had happened. There was no point in calling Chief Torbert. He wouldn't welcome the most innocent inquiry into his business. That meant she had to go stand in line at the general store. Mrs. Reed was certain to have the whole story up-to-date.

She was wrong. Agatha found only two people in the general store, and they disappeared while she was poking around for something to buy so she could engage Mary Reed in honest conversation. Peanut butter, that was it, a big jar of whipped, chunky peanut butter. She looked at the price. At $4.49 it was a dollar more than the stuff at the supermarket. Information traded high at the general store.

"Good afternoon, Mrs. Bates. Just the peanut butter?"

Agatha was sorely tempted to tell Mrs. Reed that the jar of peanut butter was all she could afford for the whole week. She settled for a comment on the sunny day outside.

"Not a good day for bad news," grumped Mrs. Reed.

"Oh. What's the bad news, Mrs. Reed?"

"The Jenkins boy. He drowned last night or late yesterday afternoon, they say."

"That's too bad," Agatha said. What appropriate remark could she make to keep Mrs. Reed talking? "How old was he?"

"Old enough to know better. No one goes in the pond this late in the year. Freeze your ears off if you dive in. The poor boy got a cramp. Dr. Parker wouldn't say what he thought it was. He could have hit his head, I suppose, but I say it was a cramp."

"I don't believe I know the Jenkinses," Agatha said apologetically.

"Donald was gone from the school yard by the time you moved in year-round. You would have heard him if he was still here." Mrs. Reed lowered her voice. "Bigmouth they called him. He was a trial to his teachers, I can tell you. They held him back twice. Then they turned him loose into the high school just to get rid of him. I heard he wasn't going back to high school this September."

"Oh, dear. Still . . ."

"I know what you mean, Mrs. Bates. That was no need for him to drown. Folks that know him say he was much improved this summer. He had an old car he'd bought. Chief Torbert said he didn't go over twenty miles an hour in it."

"His parents must be upset."

"More than upset, I can tell you," Mrs. Reed said. "He was all they had, even if he did cause them grief. I hear Mr. Jenkins is quite ill—that smoker's disease they get."

"What a terrible time for Mrs. Jenkins. I feel so sorry for her."

Mrs. Reed nodded. "I hear Sandy Prescott is staying with you until Christmas. "Is that so?" she asked.

There wasn't much that escaped Mrs. Reed's attention. As Agatha turned to reply, Mrs. Reed exclaimed, "Well, look at that. There's a state trooper. I believe he's headed to the town hall to see Chief Torbert. What do you reckon he wants, Mrs. Bates?"

"I think Chief Torbert might have given him a call," Agatha could have said. What she did say was, "I have no idea, Mrs. Reed."

·21·

Sandy hadn't been in the house ten minutes before a voice on the phone asked for "Sandy Prescott, please."

"It's for you," Agatha said. "Shall I have them call back?"

"I'll take it," Sandy said. "It's probably Cathy."

"Sandy? This is Cathy. Welcome back."

"Thanks. I haven't been gone long."

"I know, but a lot has happened. Has Agatha told you?"

"Told me what? Mom just dropped me off a minute ago and went up to our place to get some things she needs in Boston."

"About what happened to Bigmouth? Agatha hasn't told you?"

"We were talking about the yard sale."

"Bigmouth drowned, Sandy, two days ago, right there in the town pond. Wasn't it in the newspapers? It was in the Henderson papers."

"Just a second. Agatha, was there something about Bigmouth Jenkins in your Boston paper?"

"I didn't see it."

"Agatha says no," Sandy reported. "How did it happen?"

"Chief Torbert told the Jenkinses—they live next door you know—"

"I know," Sandy said.

"Chief Torbert said he must have hit his head diving off the boulder. Mom thinks he got a cramp in the cold water. A state trooper is in town to help the chief. He's been over to the Jenkins house and at the school, too. Dad says maybe it wasn't an accident. Ask Agatha what she thinks."

Sandy held the phone away from her face. "Cathy says a state trooper is in town. Her father says they may have some suspicions about what happened to Donald. She wants to know what you think."

"I don't think anything," Agatha said. Whatever she said would be passed around town with all the other gossip and rumors. Malcolm didn't need her comments from the sidelines. "Perhaps Chief Torbert and Dr. Parker are uncertain and want expert help. Dr. Parker's the one who will get state-police experts, medical examiners, and people like that."

"Hold on, Cathy," Sandy said into the phone. "What does the medical examiner do? Cathy says Chief Torbert told the Jenkinses their son was hurt on the head."

"If you're not certain about a fatal accident, the state has to look into it. That's the law."

"Agatha says the law says that you have to be certain. Your father was right, I suppose."

"Oh, boy, wait until I tell him that."

Agatha sighed. "Tell Cathy," she whispered to Sandy, "that what I told you is standard procedure. It doesn't mean anything special."

Sandy nodded. "Agatha says it's a routine procedure, Cathy. Tell your father it's nothing special."

Agatha fled into the living room. When Sandy finished,

Agatha returned to the kitchen to prepare supper. "How was the trip to the big city?" she asked.

"Great," Sandy said. "But I'm glad to be in Wingate. The city is so expensive. You wouldn't believe what Mom pays for the little two-room apartment she and Kate have. It's about half the size of the mobile home. Most places wouldn't take our dog. It's close to the park, or common, they call it. Kate can walk Duke there. We wouldn't be able to do this and take over the inn without Dad's insurance."

"You'll be moving after Christmas into a really big place," Agatha said. "It's something to look forward to. How many rooms does the inn have?"

"Lots. I don't know how many. The builder is going to make some changes. Mom is already excited."

Agatha nodded. Her mind wasn't on the inn, she realized, but what everyone else's mind in Wingate was probably on. "Tell me, Sandy, is the pond really deep? They've filled part of it in, haven't they?"

"It's deep in places, holes where you don't expect. Mostly down at this end. It's shallow at the beach, except where the big rock slides into the water; the hole there is really deep. That's where the kids dive. You have to go way down to touch bottom. It hurts your ears."

"Could Donald Jenkins have hit his head on the rock?"

"Maybe," Sandy replied. "I don't think anyone ever has. It drops off sharp there. I don't see how, unless he was coming up and bumped into it."

That was something Agatha hadn't thought of. She could imagine Donald pushing his way to the surface out of breath and stunning himself and, half-conscious, drowning. That must have occurred to Malcolm right away. She changed the subject. "How is the Graveyard Gang, did Cathy say?" she asked.

"Fine, I guess. Cathy says Amy wasn't in school today. She was getting a cold yesterday. We're going to send flowers to the Jenkinses. We have a surplus in the club budget."

Agatha's thoughts drifted to Amy Abbott. Should she call to see how Amy was getting along? She'd let Sandy do that. She had the guilty feeling it wasn't the dead teenager she was fretting about. It was Amy *and* the teenager she had locked together in her thoughts. Was it possible Amy came across his body in the lake Monday afternoon and, terrified, fled? There was no point in speculating. Sooner or later she'd find out from Chief Torbert—or from Mrs. Reed.

· 22 ·

Agatha spread the Boston paper on the table. Six sections today, no wonder we're running out of trees. Why can't they give us only two sections, the way they used to? she asked herself. Agatha poured herself a second cup of coffee and found the page with news from New England. Nothing from Wingate. Poor Donald Jenkins never got beyond the local gossip before he became no news at all.

The knock at the front door shook the house. The door shuddered and refused to move as someone pushed it. A harder push and a gruff voice sounding through the house. "Agatha, you there?"

"I'm here, Malcolm. Give the door a kick at the bottom."

Torbert came in and slumped onto the sofa. He reached underneath the cushion. "Feels like I broke a spring."

"It's been broken for years. Like everything else in this old place, including the owner. I'll get you a cup of coffee."

The chief sat up to sip his coffee. He didn't speak. That wasn't like Malcolm Torbert, Agatha thought. He moves straight to the point. Something's wrong, and he can't bring himself to say it. Poor Malcolm. He must think I'm waiting to steal his murder case. "No, Malcolm," she said, "I did not see anyone go down to the pond Monday afternoon. Is that what you wanted to know?" That should take care of it for a while, and I won't have to say that I *did* see someone come up from the beach.

Torbert held out his cup. "Do you have any left?" he asked.

Agatha took the cup. "I'll make a fresh pot. It will be ready in a few minutes." Malcolm was getting off to a slow start. She couldn't resist making one more remark. "You have a state cop out and around, do you?"

"Lieutenant Vincent Sansone. He's at the lab in Henderson right now," Torbert answered.

So that was it. Malcolm had a possible murder on his hands. Dr. Parker must have had some questions that he couldn't answer. Now Torbert and the state cop were getting the answers. Agatha said nothing. When the coffee was ready, she filled a big plastic mug. Malcolm put it on the table. He took a pack of cigarettes from his pocket, shook one out, sniffed it, crumbled it up, and emptied his hand into a wastebasket. Malcolm had been doing that as long as Agatha had known him.

"It looks like the Jenkins boy had a little help with his accident. Sansone has gone to the capital for the autopsy report."

Not a word from Agatha.

"He was struck on top of the head, which looked to me like he ran into the boulder and passed out and drowned." Malcolm paused. "He had a worse whack in the back of his head, which split his skull. That one killed him. Doc Parker and I didn't see it at first under the thick hair back there. We were paying attention to the big bump on top. The water had washed away the blood. Doc Parker and I agreed it was an accident, and that's what I told the Jenkinses. Then, when we were turning him over to the undertaker, the doctor put his hand under the boy's head and realized what had happened."

Malcolm had come by to talk, Agatha thought. "It wasn't your fault," she assured him.

"I reckon it was, Agatha. It's my business to find these things out."

"You said Parker didn't discover it right away, either."

"No matter. Sansone would have found it."

So that was it. Lieutenant Vincent Sansone had let Malcolm know he had, or almost had, made a mistake. "He's been riding you?" Agatha asked.

"Not directly, but he did suggest that the state people should be called at the beginning when there's an accident like that. And he let me know he'd take charge of any homicide investigation, if there was one. He'd be in charge, anyway; he didn't have to tell me. I'm thinking about retiring, Agatha. I've been doing this job for twenty years. It's time to move out. What's it like being a retired cop?"

"Don't let it bother you," Agatha advised.

"The boy was killed. I told his parents he had an accident. Then I told them we weren't certain. Now I have to tell them Donald was murdered. Doc Parker and I are going to look pretty dumb. You know how people talk."

"The doctor made the mistake, and you know it. How long has he been coroner?"

"Years, twenty-five maybe. He gets a drowning in one of the towns around here every year, usually a broken neck. A swimmer knocks himself out diving into a rock and drowns. That's what the doc and I figured. The body was a few feet from the beach, like he tried to reach shore. Now it looks like someone hit him and dumped him in the pond.

We can't be sure yet. There was that downpour Monday night."

"The storm didn't slam his head against the rock?"

"No way. Sansone thinks they will find his lungs are clear. Donald was probably killed on dry land."

"What was the boy doing at the pond?" Agatha asked Torbert. "It was cold and raw."

"That's what I asked the Jenkinses when I broke the news. He was a big boy, he did pretty much as he pleased. They were worried when he didn't come home, but not enough to call me. He's been swimming at the pond ever since he could walk. He worked on that old car he'd bought in the mornings and went to the beach in the afternoons. Last days of summer, I guess. I used to swim down there in October," Malcolm bragged.

"On cold, wet days?"

"No," the chief confessed.

It wasn't going to take Torbert and Sansone long to find out about Amy and Donald Jenkins. "He had a friend there?" Agatha asked tentatively.

"Maybe. He didn't have many friends. The Whitman boy was his closest. Strange kid. A hermit like his father. We asked him first. He hadn't seen Donald since a little after school got out last June. The Jenkins boy worked all summer over in Coldstream."

"I doubt it's going to take you long to find out who hit him. It was probably a disagreement that got out of hand. Maybe they were drunk." Agatha had heard from Mrs. Reed that there were some crazy teenagers in Wingate who drank too much beer.

"A hell of a disagreement," Torbert said.

96

Agatha was silent. She had the feeling Torbert wasn't telling her *all* the details of the murder.

"We have a couple of things," Malcolm went on. "When his mother asked him where he was going Monday, Donald told her he had to see his princess. And in the front seat of the car was a girl's rain jacket, bright pink."

Dear God, Agatha said to herself. Could it be Amy's? She shook her head and bent over the coffeepot to hide her anguish. "Here's the last of it, Malcolm. Another pot?"

Torbert shook his head. "No, thanks. I have to be on my way. See you, Agatha."

·23·

Thursday morning Paul reached down to shake Amy gently by the shoulder. "School today?" he asked.

Amy groaned, "I don't know. I'll see."

"Unless you're really sick, I don't think you'd better miss another day. Teachers like to see enthusiasm the first weeks of school."

Amy felt the tension seeping through her body. Her shoulders were stiff, her legs didn't want to move, her hands were closed into fists, and her head began to throb.

"Should we make an appointment with Dr. Parker?"

"No!" Amy almost shouted. She sat up and stuffed her feet into her slippers. Dr. Parker's office, Cathy had told her, was where they had taken Donald. Dr. Parker would look at her and shake his head. He would suspect. Doctors could tell things just by looking at you. Amy went to the bathroom and waited for the warm water to come through the pipes. She pressed a warm washcloth to her face. Paul was right, she had to go to school. What was she afraid of? So what if someone found out that she and Donald had met and talked on the beach? There wasn't anything wrong with that. Paul would be hurt that she'd lied to him, but he wouldn't tell Mom. He didn't want to upset her any more than Amy did.

She had made up her mind, anyway, Amy told herself, that she wouldn't see Bigmouth again, even if he didn't go down south. Her real friends were back. They would be busy keeping the club going. Sandy would be in school today. They would ask Mr. LaGrange if they could make the plans for the school Halloween party. Someday after the fuss died down, she might, she just might, call on the Jenkinses to tell them how sorry she was about what had happened to Donald.

Already the memory of last week had faded. It wasn't like when Dad had been hit at the corner of Walnut and the other street. What was it called? Crosby, that was it, the corner of Walnut and Crosby. Two quiet streets, anyone would have thought, where you could ride your bike in the middle of the street without worrying about cars. The three kids in the stolen pickup hadn't even lived close-by. They were speeding through the crossing, never stopping to see what was coming. Amy shuddered. Bigmouth Jenkins faded from her mind.

"There was an early frost up here on the hill," Paul said.

"Up here on the hill?" Amy asked. Bigmouth had said they would be getting frost soon.

"Twenty-eight degrees at six o'clock. I decided not to jog until I had you in school. Are you all right?"

"I think so," Amy replied. "It must have been the twenty-four-hour bug that's going around. And I was worried about Mom." That wasn't so. The only thought she had given to Mom was to worry that she might hear about Donald and her. When she was grown-up and off in college and Mom was in good shape, she would tell her about the week at the town beach with Wingate's misfit. Would she have forgotten Bigmouth altogether by then?

I'll wear my pink windbreaker, she decided. I've never worn it to school. It's nothing special. The kids won't hold it against me. I'll cut off the label.

The jacket wasn't in the drawer where it had been since Mom bought it for her last September. Puzzled, Amy looked in the closet. Not there, either. It must be at Agatha's. She must have worn it to her house one of those drippy days last week. She ran down the stairs, grabbing her denim jacket off the peg. "See you," she shouted to Paul. "I may be home late."

Did Malcolm Torbert have something else on his mind this morning? Agatha asked herself. Or had he dropped by to talk to a fellow officer? Did he know Amy Abbott had been here last week? Amy must have seen the Jenkins boy at the lake. Had she pulled him ashore to find him dead and fled? No, she decided. She wouldn't have run away from school Tuesday afternoon the way she did. She hadn't known Donald was dead. Was she running home Monday because they had quarreled and Amy had whacked him with a rock? Maybe he had assaulted her. But she wouldn't have dumped him into the water. That wouldn't have occurred to her.

Poor Amy. Agatha imagined her trying to stand up to Lieutenant Sansone's questions. The girl remembered everything about her father's accident, the cars, the ambulance, the police, the whole traumatic event. Now, another accident, a dead boyfriend. Not just a boyfriend, in Amy's eyes—a forbidden boyfriend. Could she take it?

Agatha rummaged on the sewing machine for the phone

directory. You shouldn't do this, she told herself, you are meddling. Sansone will be furious if he finds out. Let him find out, Agatha muttered. I mustn't let him terrify an insecure young girl into collapse. "Mr. Bruce," she said to the answering voice. "This is Agatha Bates. Amy was helping me the past week clear out my cellar."

"Yes. Amy said you would help us sell some of the junk in our basement." The man's voice was calm, collected, controlled. "I've made a list, though I'm afraid Amy has gone off without it. I'll bring it by sometime today if that's convenient."

"Perhaps I could pick it up," Agatha said, relieved that she could talk out of sight with the stepfather. "I'm on my way to Winthrop. I'll take the old road."

"I'll be pleased to meet Amy's new friend," Paul Bruce said graciously.

An hour later Agatha sat across from Paul Bruce in the sunny, big kitchen of the Bruce house. "That's about it," she said. "I am out of bounds being here. I did feel that Amy's health was more important than Sansone's surprise."

Paul Bruce tapped an index finger on his lower teeth. "The lieutenant won't harass her. I'll answer for that. Amy is not as fragile as she appears, but who can say what memories and fears all this will release? I can only wish she had brought herself to tell me about the Jenkins boy. It will be harder for her to tell me now. I didn't even know about the drowning. I seldom go to Wingate; we generally shop in Coldstream. My wife has rather strong opinions about Wingate." Paul Bruce smiled faintly.

"I understand. I am an outsider, too. After thirty summers and a full year and another summer, I am still an outsider. But it's a nice town, as your wife will find out if she's patient."

101

"I'm sure you're right. As I told Amy and Stephen, it's not the town that is at fault. We will have to keep all this from Kitty until she is stronger. You know, Mrs. Bates, I am not a careless parent. On the one hand I did think it odd Amy would go swimming this late in the year, especially when the weather turned nasty, but she is a wonderful swimmer. On the other hand I was pleased she was with you and, I supposed, with a friend at the beach. Only it was someone she didn't tell me about, and now some police officers are going to reveal her secret, and I can't stop them. Should I have an attorney available, Mrs. Bates?"

"No, but if Sansone goes beyond reasonable limits, you must step in. Tell him he's gone far enough, and if he intends to come back, to call you beforehand and you will have your attorney present."

"I understand. It will not be improper if I call a lawyer today for advice?"

"By no means. I am sorry that Amy didn't tell me about the boy. I felt that we had what people these days call a good relationship."

"It wasn't you, Mrs. Bates. She was protecting her mother—or herself from her mother. A little of both, I think. Neither Amy nor her mother was ready to deal with Big-mouth Jenkins."

·24·

"Were you all right at school?" Paul asked the minute Amy came into the house.

"I was okay. Sandy was back. We had a quick meeting of the Graveyard Gang. We're going to plan a Halloween party at school. And we're sending flowers to the Jenkinses. Wilma is in charge of that."

"The boy who was drowned?" Paul asked innocently. "He hit his head, is that what happened?"

"I guess so," Amy mumbled. "I have a lot of homework. It's not my night for supper, is it?"

"No, it's mine. Wasn't Donald Jenkins the one you called Bigmouth, the one who dropped the cat from the tree?"

"Yes," Amy replied, and edged toward the door.

"Was he at the beach last week when you were there?" Paul asked.

Amy shook her head. She made it to the stairs. "Ring the bell when supper is ready."

"Our teacher is really nice," Amy reported at the supper table. "She's Canadian. We're really going to have to work hard this year. And we'll start French, she said, only those who want it. It will be in our free period." Keep talking,

103

Amy told herself. No more questions about Bigmouth. All over the school kids were talking about what had happened to Donald. Cathy had mentioned about fifty times that she lived right next door. The state-police officer made two visits to the Jenkinses yesterday. Cathy's dad said the detective was on to something. "Wouldn't it be something if he questioned the Graveyard Gang?" Cathy had chattered. "Wouldn't that be something?"

A car was pulling to the top of the driveway. You could see the lights through the kitchen window. Who could that be? Almost no one ever came up to the house, never in the evenings. It must be someone to see Paul. The lights went out, a car door slammed, and there were steps on the outside stairs. A firm knock sounded at the door. Amy saw Paul grimace when he got up, as though he were expecting a visitor he didn't want to talk to.

Opening the door, Paul said, "Yes?"

"Could I come in, please?" a voice asked. "Lieutenant Sansone, New Hampshire State Police. My I.D."

"Come in," Paul said.

The officer entered the kitchen. He smiled briefly at Amy. Lieutenant Sansone was a slender man, not very tall, with short black hair. He didn't look friendly to Amy, certainly not like Chief Torbert, who had a big smile for everyone. She felt nervous. He must be here to ask about Bigmouth, just the way Cathy had said he might.

"I'm looking into the death of Donald Jenkins." The officer was talking to Paul. "Chief Torbert and I are trying to find out a few things about the boy."

"I've heard that he drowned," said Paul, who for once didn't sound overpolite.

104

"Yes. Still, we have to look into accidents we can't be certain about."

"There is a question, then, about his death?" Paul asked, now in control of his calm, quiet voice.

The lieutenant didn't answer directly. "I'd like to ask your daughter a couple of questions, if that's all right, sir."

"What do you say, Amy?"

"I guess so," Amy said hesitantly. Now she was really scared. Well, she had already made up her mind, she wasn't going to tell *anyone* about Donald. That was her secret.

"You knew Donald Jenkins?"

Amy nodded. "Sort of," she replied.

"Sort of?"

"Excuse me," Paul interrupted. "I'll clear off the table." He picked up the plates and the macaroni dish. "Sit down, Lieutenant. You too, Amy."

Lieutenant Sansone took a chair across the table from Amy. He looked at her steadily. "What do you mean 'sort of'?"

"Coffee, Lieutenant?" Paul asked.

He's trying to help me, Amy thought. "He wasn't in school or anything. I've only been here for a year, a little longer, maybe. My friends knew him better. They talked about him sometimes."

"How? What did they say?"

"I don't remember much, that he failed in school and talked in a loud voice, something like that."

"Nothing else?" Sansone insisted.

"Nothing I can think of."

"Aren't you forgetting about the cat, Amy?" Paul interrupted again.

"Could I ask the questions, Mr. Abbott?" Sansone asked sharply.

"Not Abbott, Bruce. Paul Bruce. Amy is my stepdaughter."

"Stepdaughter, yes. I'll remember that, Mr. Bruce. What cat was your stepfather talking about, Amy?"

"I forgot about that. We were having a club meeting on the graveyard wall, and Bigmouth, I mean Donald, was up in the tree. We didn't see him, and he dropped a dead cat down on top of us. We were scared. Then he laughed at us. It was his mother's cat, I think. He was supposed to bury it."

"I see. Nothing else?"

"Not that I can think of."

"How about the time he scared you into jumping off the road?"

"How did you know?" Amy asked.

The officer didn't answer. He hadn't taken his eyes off her since they sat down.

"He came up behind Sandy and me, in his father's car, I guess. We were walking on the wrong side of the road. He blew his horn and we jumped."

"That's all?"

"He told us to walk facing traffic."

"That's all?"

There was that other time when Donald came up behind her at the bottom of the driveway. The man seemed to know everything. She'd better not leave that out. "He did that again, maybe a week later. He came up alongside me at the driveway and wanted to know if I was going up to 'the palace.' He knew I lived here, I guess."

"I see. Nothing else?"

106

"No."

"No phone calls?"

"I would know about that, Lieutenant," Paul said. "There were no phone calls. Could you tell me what you're getting at?"

"Doing my job, Mr. Bruce. No phone calls here, I should have said. How about phone calls to the Spruce Tree Lodge?"

"Those? I don't know who it was. The guy didn't say. My friends and I thought it might be Donald Jenkins. After a while they stopped."

"You didn't tell me about them," Sansone said. He sounded accusing.

"Do you have some evidence those calls were made by the boy who drowned?" Paul demanded. "Amy told me about them. What is the point of this?"

Lieutenant Sansone paid no attention. "Do you ever swim in the town pond, Amy?" he asked.

"Sometimes."

"Like last week?"

"Yes. After I left Agatha's. We were cleaning out the cellar. I was hot and dirty."

"Wednesday, Thursday, Friday. Those were cool days."

"I didn't care. I felt like swimming before I went home. Exercise, I guess."

"The water was cold, wasn't it?"

"Real cold," Amy agreed.

"Anyone at the beach?"

Amy shook her head.

"And Monday was cold, too. Did you go to the beach that day?"

"No," Amy said.

"That's it, then." Sansone stood up. "Thank you very much, Amy. And thank you, Mr. Bruce." He held out his hand to Paul. "Sorry to have bothered you. We're trying to clean up a few loose ends." He walked to the door. He pulled it open. "Oh," he suddenly said. "I forgot." He turned toward Amy and Paul. He had a pink rain jacket in his hand.

Amy jumped to her feet. "It's my jacket. Where did you find it?" Now she remembered. She must have dropped it on the beach—or in Bigmouth's old car. Amy sank back into the chair. She looked at Paul, fear frozen in her face. "I want to go up to my room. I can't answer anymore. I have to go to bed."

"We've had enough questions, Lieutenant," Paul said coldly. "I'm certain you will be back. Please call me before you come. I will want to consult my attorney."

"That is your privilege, Mr. Bruce." Sansone closed the door behind him.

·25·

Bigmouth Jenkins finally made it into the Boston newspaper. Three lines in the New England section of Friday's paper reported that Donald Jenkins, drowning victim in Wingate, New Hampshire, had been murdered and state police were undertaking an investigation. Now I won't have to bother Malcolm and Mrs. Reed, Agatha thought. She could imagine the shock waves passing through the town. There was bound to be a long story in the Henderson newspaper, which liked nothing better than front-page stories about gory automobile accidents and local murders. By now every copy in the general store would be sold out. She would have to rely on Channel Nine News. Their people must be in town by now.

Poor Amy. And poor Malcolm Torbert, made to feel like a country bumpkin. He might just resign after all; the chief was a proud man. Could Amy have knocked Bigmouth in the head? Agatha asked herself again. The idea was preposterous. Still, over half her life, she had to admit, had been spent in dealing with preposterous situations, things you had trouble believing even after you had seen them with your own eyes. Amy had grabbed a rock and for whatever reason had hit Donald Jenkins twice, once on the top of his head and again, in the back of his head, hard enough this time to fracture his skull. Or maybe in reverse order.

Agatha could not visualize that. Jenkins was a big strong boy, Torbert had said. He had his back to Amy? Where? In the lake? That was impossible. In the car then, not with a rock but some sort of tool. From the backseat or from under her feet, Amy had reached and grabbed something hard and smashed the unsuspecting Donald. No one would sit still for that, Agatha argued. Amy didn't murder the boy, she was altogether convinced. At the same time she understood perfectly that Lieutenant Vincent Sansone could see how Amy might have done the deed in at least half a dozen different ways.

A rich-looking car stopped on the street outside. A tall, bespectacled man in a red sweater got out and came across the lawn to the door. And here I am in my ratty old bathrobe, Agatha realized. She took the door off the latch. "Come in," she called to Paul Bruce. "I'll be right back."

Suitably dressed, Agatha brought Amy's stepfather a cup of coffee. The man wasted no time in apologizing. "I came by as soon as I was sure Amy was in school. She insisted on walking. The Mercedes is a big embarrassment to her, I'm afraid."

Agatha smiled. "Kids have to be the same as other kids these days."

"The officer you warned me about showed up last night. He behaved precisely the way you predicted. Tough, and at the end, nasty."

"He has to do his job, Mr. Bruce. Was Chief Torbert with him?"

"No, he came alone."

110

Agatha didn't say that Malcolm was in disgrace. "How did Amy take it?"

"Rather well, I thought. It's surprising how efficiently children can lie, much better than adults. At the end, Sansone got to her, and she almost broke down. He showed her a jacket."

"A jacket?" Agatha asked.

"A pink nylon windbreaker. It was hers, Amy admitted. I had never seen it before. It was probably one of the things Kitty had bought that Amy didn't wear because it wasn't right. She would only wear it to an empty beach. That's when I stopped Sansone, Mrs. Bates."

"Agatha, please."

"Yes. Agatha it is. Did you see her wear a rain jacket last week?"

"No, I didn't, I'm quite sure. The cold days, Thursday and Friday, she kept her sweatshirt on, a Harvard sweatshirt."

"That was Harry's—her father's. It's very special. She won't wash it."

"I thought it might be. Did you ask her about the windbreaker?"

"This morning. Last night she had enough questions. I gave her two aspirin and tucked her in. But this morning, I did ask," Paul went on. "Amy said she thought that she may have left it at your place last Friday, but that it must have been at the beach and someone had picked it up. She was positive she didn't go to the beach Monday afternoon. She was lying, wasn't she?"

"Protecting herself, you might say, or her mother," Agatha explained. "She doesn't want to upset anyone, and

111

she's afraid. It was probably Amy I saw running across the field last Monday."

"You didn't tell me," Paul accused Agatha.

"I didn't tell Chief Torbert, either, Mr. Bruce. If I'd been certain I would have been obliged to tell him. Amy told Vincent she was at the pond every afternoon last week, but not Monday?"

"Yes."

"But she didn't see Donald Jenkins?"

"That is what she said."

"I don't believe that Sansone will accept that Donald Jenkins found a pink jacket and put it in his car."

"Sansone didn't say where he found it."

"No, he wouldn't. But he had it, and that is where it was, you may be sure. He is thinking what I am thinking, Mr. Bruce, that Amy met Donald Jenkins every afternoon last week and probably Monday afternoon. By now he has other evidence to back it up. He will return, count on it. He may not be so polite the next time."

"Shall I have an attorney present?"

"I cannot advise you. You should talk it over with Amy and decide what is best for her. She is a juvenile; that limits what Sansone can do. She will probably stick to her story. She is stuck with it. She will convince herself what she said is true. Amy seems to fantasize."

"What will the lieutenant do?"

"Nothing, for a while. I suspect he has no idea who killed Donald Jenkins."

"I don't know how much Amy can take," Paul mused. "The talk at school, how her friends react, the gossip that will center on her. She didn't kill Donald, did she, Agatha? He didn't attack her and she killed him?"

"I don't believe so, but it's possible, I suppose. I have no idea what the boy was like."

"Someone killed him."

"Someone did, you're right. Amy will have her friends' support, Mr. Bruce."

"Paul. Call me Paul, please."

"Amy will have a tough time avoiding the truth with them. It will be too complicated for her. It's a lot easier to lie to adults. She will want to confess. Please encourage her to be with the Graveyard Gang."

Paul Bruce's thoughts seemed to be on the boy who was Amy's friend. "Who could have killed him?" he asked again.

"Someone who had a reason," Agatha replied. "There's always a reason, even if it's crazy."

"Maybe it was one of those lunatics, serial killers, who kill for no reason at all, and no one has cause to suspect them."

"Perhaps. Chief Torbert knows the town and everyone in it. He will persuade Sansone to go beyond Amy Abbott in his investigation. I will talk to the Graveyard Gang. They may have some ideas. I'll keep in touch, Paul."

·26·

"Did you see the paper, Sandy?" Cathy asked excitedly. "Mom found it right away in the Boston paper. There was something on the eleven o'clock news, too, she said."

"What about?" Sandy asked.

"Bigmouth Jenkins. He didn't drown. He was *murdered*. Can you believe it, right here in Wingate?"

"Ugh," Wilma said. "Let's not talk about it. I still have nightmares about that dead cat. Everyone in town's going to the service tomorrow. My mother said I had to go pay my respects."

"They took the body over to Henderson for an examination," Cathy said.

Wilma looked as though she was going to be sick.

"That's enough, Cathy," Sandy said. "Did you send the flowers, Wilma?"

"My mother did, and I paid her. Twenty-five-dollars' worth. There's only two dollars and thirty-five cents left in the treasury. I signed all our names on the card."

"Agatha, Amy, and I are having a big yard sale in a couple of weeks. We could sell some stuff on commission, Agatha says, if we collect it from people who have things they want to unload," Sandy explained.

"That's a good idea," Cathy said. "Mom was wishing the other day she could get rid of some of the stuff in the storeroom."

The first bell rang, and the girls drifted toward the schoolhouse. Sandy waved to Amy, who appeared at the end of Main Street. Amy was dragging her feet. "She's going to be late again," Sandy said to Cathy. "She must still be sick."

The last bell had rung when Amy pushed her way into the eighth-grade room. She slumped into a seat at the back of the room. Miss Wilder looked up from the poem she had started to read to the class, to get them settled into the proper frame of mind, she said. "Good morning, Amy. Do you think you can get here on time from now on?"

"Yes, ma'am. I'm sorry."

Miss Wilder went back to the poem. Only an hour ago, Amy thought, Paul had practically pulled her out of bed. "I don't feel well," she had protested.

"I know you don't," Paul had said, "but you have to go. That is where your friends are. I can't help you much directly, Amy. I do know that you have to face up to things when they come your way. You haven't told me whether you were friends with the poor Jenkins boy or not. The lieutenant obviously thinks you were. If you ran into him on the beach and got to be friends, that was no crime. One thing I am sure of, Amy, is that you did not harm him."

"I didn't see him, Dad." There, she finally called him Dad. "Honest, I just left my jacket there, and he must have picked it up."

"We have the weekend to talk about it, Amy. The officer will probably be back. I won't let him badger you. But to see this through you will need your friends to support you, and Agatha Bates as well. I might as well tell you that there will be talk. That's only natural in a small town. You mustn't let it upset you."

"Couldn't we move?" Amy had asked. "Mom wanted to move. That's why she's in the hospital." Paul made a face. Amy saw that she had hurt him. "I'm sorry. I didn't mean it."

"If we run away, Amy, it will be a sign something is wrong. You must understand that. There is no reason for us to leave. Friendship with Donald Jenkins was a good thing, Amy. He made a friend and so did you."

"He wasn't my friend. I never saw him at the beach, not once. You don't believe me, do you? You believe the trooper."

No more talk after that. Amy had drunk her milk, packed her lunch, and left in silence. When Paul said, "Good-bye, Amy," she did not respond.

Wilma looked over her shoulder. She moved her lips to ask, "Are you all right?" and smiled.

Amy smiled back, a sad, sick smile it must have been, she realized. Wilma was a real sweetheart. So were Cathy and Sandy. Whatever happened, even if they put her in jail, she could count on the Graveyard Gang. She wouldn't leave them, Amy decided. Paul was right. They had to stay. She could never find friends like Sandy, Cathy, and Wilma anywhere else. Suddenly, Amy realized that Miss Wilder was talking to her. "I'm sorry. I didn't hear," Amy confessed. Miss Wilder frowned. She was getting mad now. Amy forced herself to pay attention.

At lunchtime they settled under the big sugar maple in the side school yard. "Peanut butter and jelly again," Wilma groaned. "You'd think after seven years my mother would learn there are other kinds of sandwiches."

"Agatha made us a cake," Sandy said proudly, unfolding

the aluminum foil. "Only it didn't rise. It's a flat cake," she laughed, "but it tastes all right. Agatha is learning to cook."

"Hey," Cathy spoke up. "I have a great idea. We can have a bake sale at the yard sale. How about that? With hot chocolate and cider."

"Good idea," Sandy said. "We'll put up signs. Agatha said to come by after soccer, Amy. Are you playing this year?"

"I'd like to start on Monday," Amy said. "I'm still feeling weak. Maybe I'll come down to see you and Agatha Saturday or Sunday."

"How'd it go, Amy?" Paul asked as soon as Amy came in the door.

"Okay. I have to do the homework for the day I missed. Miss Wilder said I have to keep up."

"Good idea," Paul agreed.

When the phone rang toward five o'clock, Paul shouted up the steps. "It's your friend Cathy."

"Amy, you'll never guess," Cathy began. "Chief Torbert and the state trooper are talking to the Graveyard Gang. Can you imagine? They questioned Wilma, next me, and I bet they're going to see Sandy and you. I told you they might talk to us, remember?"

"What did they ask?" Amy asked fearfully.

"Oh, about the cat, and if Bigmouth had bothered us other times. And about that creepy Perry Whitman. And what did we know about the phone calls you got. I told the officer— he's the one with all the questions—straight out we thought it was Bigmouth. I mean Donald."

"Maybe it was someone else. We weren't certain."

"It was Donald who called you Princess, wasn't it?"

117

"Yes." Amy felt her heart beat faster.

"That's what I told him. Those phone calls were for the princess. That's who he asked for, Milly said, remember? It had to be Donald."

"I don't remember," Amy said softly. "Maybe it was."

"They'll be up to see you, next, I bet. I thought I'd tell you. Isn't it exciting?"

·27·

Long after midnight Amy finally went to sleep. Dream followed dream, all different, all very ordinary, pushing her into wakefulness. Toward dawn she fell into an undisturbed slumber.

"You had two phone calls," Paul said, "from Cathy and Wilma. I don't believe I've talked to Wilma before. She sounds very nice."

"She is," Amy said. She bent over and scratched Crutch behind the ears. "How about a walk, Crutch? It's cool out, isn't it?" she asked Paul.

"Another frost last night. I have to go to Coldstream. Anything we need from the store?"

"Cheese, not too sharp. I'm making rarebit. And raisins for the rice pudding. I can't think of anything else."

"Fine. How about a movie?"

"I can't. Miss Wilder loads us up on weekends. I'll take Crutch to the river and get started on my math."

"Don't forget to call your friends."

"I won't. Come on, Crutch."

The old dog limped to the driveway. He looked back to see where they were headed. He followed Amy toward the meadow. A brisk wind moved through the knee-high grass.

119

The path to the river was almost invisible. We haven't been this way since last spring, Amy thought. How long ago that was, how much had happened since then. She could scarcely remember back to the Saturday after school when she and her friends had formed the Graveyard Gang and worked those two months at the lodge. Those days seemed like centuries ago. Now all of the past was contained in a week—and a day!—at the pond.

Bigmouth wasn't real anymore. Try as she might, Amy couldn't picture him completely in her mind. He was only bits and pieces: the dark eyes; the thick curl of hair at the back of his head, where they said he was hit; the purple bruised thumb he hurt at the Sunoco station; those filthy sneakers with the laces flopping around his legs.

I better not think about it, Amy told herself. I don't want to know any more. Today or tomorrow Sansone would be coming back, she was certain. She'd tell him the same thing. She wasn't going to tell him about Donald. The officer wouldn't understand. *Princess,* the word echoed. "See you tomorrow, Princess?" and "Take care, Princess," and, at the end, "Come back, Princess. Hey, wait a minute, Princess, I'm sorry." That was what he had said, he was sorry. They were the very last words she heard as she took off as fast as she could run. "Hey, Princess, wait a minute. I'm sorry."

Crutch nosed ahead, sniffing in the grass for animal smells, for a deer or, more likely, a woodchuck. In the spring when the grass had been flattened by the snow, you could see their burrows. Whole families lived in the field, Paul said. Had Donald shot woodchuck, too? You can't eat them, Amy thought. It must have been only deer. That's what they shot,

Bigmouth and his dad, deer, but only the bucks, he'd assured Amy.

Crutch came to the river's edge and looked back for permission to go in. The Wincatesset was a wide, flat river most of the year, half rock and half running streams pushing among the boulders. "Go get 'em, Crutch," Amy shouted. She threw a piece of driftwood out into a pool of water. Crutch walked out to where the stream came to his belly. He stopped and barked once at the driftwood floating downstream beyond him.

"I'm not going to get it for you." Amy laughed. "Go get it yourself." She threw another piece of wood, which splashed a few feet beyond the dog. Crutch took two steps and watched the wood drift away. Then he turned around and plodded ashore. He shook himself and sat beside Amy. Amy threw a stone as far as she could. It skipped once and disappeared. Crutch stood up and barked.

"You silly," Amy shouted. For the first time in days she felt good. Amy leaned against a log the spring torrents had thrown far up onto the shore. Crutch flattened out at her feet and shut his eyes. Amy lifted her face to the morning sun. Her problems drained away. "I'll be all right," she told herself. "I'll be all right, won't I, Crutch?" She had to stay away from Paul until she was safe. He knew she was not telling the truth about what happened. He wanted to help her, but she had to stay away from him for a while, from the others, too. After a while, everything would go away. People would forget. I'll be all right. Amy rose to her feet. "Come on, Crutch. It's homework time."

The phone kept ringing through the early afternoon. Amy pretended she didn't hear. Finally the ringing stopped. Amy heard Paul enter the kitchen. The rustle of paper bags told her he was putting away the groceries. Afterward, steps at the bottom of the front stairs. "Are you all right?" he called.

"Sure. I'm doing my homework. There's a lot of it." There wasn't, really. She had finished most of it. She could take a nap or read a book until supper.

"I bought frozen food," Paul answered. "I'll pop it into the microwave any time you're ready."

"Okay."

"Did you call your friends?"

"There wasn't any answer."

"They must have gone to the funeral. I figured that was why they were calling."

The funeral service! The gang was going to the funeral service at the United Church. They were to meet at Wilma's house, which was closest to the church. Amy pushed her chair back. I'm losing my mind, she thought, like after Dad died. I couldn't pay attention. It's getting to be like that time. Amy closed her eyes and raised her head toward the ceiling. I have to pay attention, she told herself. I must, I must.

"Amy?" the voice was halfway up the steps. Paul entered her room. "What is it?" he asked. He was upset, she could tell. His voice was saying, "Tell me, Amy. What's wrong?"

"I forgot, Dad. I forgot. We all planned to go to Donald's service. I forgot." Or I didn't want to go, she thought. I went to the river and sat in the sun and forgot. I must have blocked.

Paul sat on the bed. "You have to let it out, Amy. It will get worse. If you can't talk to me, perhaps you can talk with Mrs. Bates. I can't help you, Amy, unless I know what happened. You can't avoid it forever. Lieutenant Sansone won't let you."

Amy sat up straight and made herself face Paul. I can't, she thought. I tell him and I'll have to tell everyone. I won't be able to take that. She stood up, still looking at Paul. "I have to go to the bathroom," she said.

As she splashed water on her face, Amy heard the phone ring. She pulled the door shut. It wasn't for her. She heard the sound, not the words, of Paul answering, in his usual voice. Somebody else was doing most of the talking. Amy cracked the door to hear. Was it Sansone? "I'll get her," she heard Paul say. Amy pulled the door shut.

Paul tapped on the door. "It's your mother. She'd like to talk to you."

"Mom? I'll be right there. Is she okay?"

"She sounds fine."

"Hello? Is that you, Mom?" Amy said.

"It is, honey, the one and only. Don't ask me how I am. It's been a rest for me. That's what I needed, I think, a rest."

"That's great, Mom. I've been meaning to write, but I didn't have anything to say. I will from now on, every weekend. I'll write on one of your note cards. The sea gulls, maybe. That was the one Wilma bought for her mother's birthday."

Mom's voice changed. Impatient, maybe angry. "No, none of those. And not a postcard from Wingate, New Hampshire, either. Remember that boy, that Bigmouth boy? The one in Stephen's school bus?"

Amy held her breath. "I guess so, Mom."

"You guess so, Amy? You just guess so? He got himself killed in some fight or something, and you just guess so? I read it in the paper. That's why I called. To tell Paul to get you out of that town. Now!" Mom was screeching. "Put Paul on the phone. I want to talk to him," she shouted.

There was silence on the phone. Then a cool, calm voice told Amy that he was Dr. Farber and he'd call back tomorrow.

·28·

"It was a short service, was it?" Agatha asked when Sandy returned in the middle of Saturday afternoon.

"The preacher only said a few words," Sandy replied.

"Was Amy there?" Agatha asked.

"No. Cathy and Wilma both called her. She was supposed to call back, but she never did."

"Perhaps she felt she didn't know the Jenkins boy well enough," Agatha suggested. "I mean, she's new in Wingate. Having a dead cat dropped on you isn't much of an introduction."

Sandy stared at Agatha for a long while, making up her mind to speak. "Amy knew him all right," she said at last. "Mrs. Jenkins has been saying she was the one who killed Donald, according to Cathy."

"No," Agatha said in disbelief.

"It's true. That's what she told Mrs. Cameron and some other people. 'The Princess,' she calls her—just like I heard Bigmouth call Amy—'that rich princess up on the hill is the one who took my boy from me.'"

"She was upset, Sandy, probably hysterical."

"That's what she said, not once but a couple of times.

That's why Cathy was calling Amy, to tell her it would be better if she didn't come to the service."

Dear God, Agatha thought. What a way for things to come out. "The chief and Lieutenant Sansone were at the church?" she asked.

"Standing at the back, next to us. When the Jenkinses followed the coffin out, Mrs. Jenkins went up to them and said something like, 'What are you going to do about it? You know she did it. She killed my boy.' Mr. Jenkins had to pull her away."

"You girls don't think Amy had anything to do with it, do you?"

"Of course not. It had to be someone pretty strong, people say." Sandy paused, debating whether to go on. "The police seem pretty certain she was at the beach, or Mrs. Jenkins wouldn't be talking the way she is. That's what Cathy's folks say, anyway. Mrs. Schrader saw a boy and girl there one afternoon, she doesn't know who. And Donald told his folks he was going to the beach on Monday to see his princess. We heard they found a girl's jacket, too."

"I see," Agatha said. Now she was the one who hesitated. Finally she admitted, "I think she was there, too, but I'm certain she wasn't the one who hit Donald."

"But who?" Sandy asked. "Nobody's talking about anyone except Amy Abbott, about whether she did or didn't."

"I have no idea," Agatha said.

"When Lieutenant Sansone talked to Cathy, Wilma, and me yesterday afternoon about the Graveyard Gang, you could tell he was mostly interested in Amy."

Agatha shook her head. "I think Donald and another boy had a fight about something and Donald was struck."

"But who?" Sandy asked again.

126

And again Agatha had to reply, "I have no idea."

"Can't you help Chief Torbert?"

"Sandy, the police are better equipped than I am. Chief Torbert knows everyone in Wingate. They don't need me."

"Why doesn't Amy tell the police she was at the beach with him if she was?"

"Why do you think?" Agatha asked.

"Yeah, I know. Her mother is in a mental hospital, and she's trying to get along in school, and Donald Jenkins isn't the sort of guy you'd want people to think was your boyfriend."

"You and your friends may be able to help."

"How? We'll do whatever we can," Sandy said.

"Give Amy all the support you can. Let her know she's your friend and you believe in her. Encourage her to talk to us and to Chief Torbert."

"I figured you to be checking in sooner or later, Agatha," Torbert said. "Once a cop always a cop, I've always said. Another cup of coffee, please. Are you bringing Sandy up to be the next chief of police? I heard she was studying to run the Wingate Inn."

"We haven't named it yet," Sandy told him.

"It doesn't matter what you name it, Sandy, everyone will keep on calling it the Wingate Inn. Now, what is it you want, Agatha? Something about the Abbott girl, I reckon."

"First, what I don't want is to meddle, Malcolm."

"That's fine with me, Agatha. I'm having enough trouble with Sansone."

Agatha was tempted to tell Torbert that Sansone had no business sharing evidence with a distraught mother, but she held her tongue. "Amy Abbott was at the pond last week, probably talking to a boy, who, it turns out, was probably Donald Jenkins.''

"You didn't tell me that earlier, Agatha."

"I wasn't certain. And that would have been meddling. It was something I felt at the time, nothing Amy told me. Apparently you and Sansone have found out some things to tell Mrs. Jenkins which seem to have led her to accuse Amy Abbott of murder."

Malcolm Torbert sipped his coffee. He looked at Sandy. "You and your friends heard her, did you?"

Sandy nodded.

"It wasn't my doing, Agatha," Torbert muttered.

"I didn't suppose it was," she said. "Amy's father will most likely have an attorney present the next time Sansone calls."

"I reckon," Malcolm said.

"But that won't keep Amy from being destroyed by gossip and accusations, will it?"

Chief Torbert shrugged. "I can't help that. The girl won't talk to us."

"You know about her father and her mother both?" Agatha asked.

"Sort of. Saw how her father was killed in a hit-and-run, and her mother is in a hospital."

"Right. How do you suppose she feels, Malcolm?"

The chief stood up. "You're meddling, Agatha."

"Only with Amy Abbott, Chief Torbert. Sandy and I and a couple of girls in a club called the Graveyard Gang will try to persuade Amy to tell you what she knows."

"Sansone is determined to have another talk with her."

"With less success than before, I would imagine. What do

you say, Malcolm? Let's give the girl a chance to tell you in her own way in her own time. In the meantime . . ."

"In the meantime we should get on with finding the person who actually murdered Donald Jenkins, is that what you were going to say, Agatha?"

"You said it, Malcolm, not me. You're the cop."

·29·

A few minutes before Sunday noon Lieutenant Sansone called.

"Will it be all right if I come by to ask Amy a few questions?" he asked politely. He wasn't friendly, but he didn't sound quite as harsh as he had Thursday night.

"It's Sunday, Lieutenant," Paul replied.

"I realize it's Sunday, Mr. Bruce. I have to work on weekends, unfortunately."

"There are some ugly rumors going around town, Lieutenant. I have the notion, perhaps mistaken, that you may be responsible for them."

"There have been rumors in every murder case I have ever worked on, Mr. Bruce. It goes with the job. I can only say I am sorry."

"Then I will have to deal with them myself," Paul said crisply. "I am of two minds, frankly, about your questioning Amy again without an attorney present. My inclination is to let her stick it out on her own, because I am certain she has nothing substantial to hide. But I cannot allow you to run over her. And I cannot allow whatever she says to you to become public gossip."

"At this stage it's only between the girl and me, Mr. Bruce.

Chief Torbert and I believe she can tell us some things which we need to know. I think Amy, for whatever reason, is withholding information."

"I will ask her," Paul said. "Can you call back in a few minutes?"

"I can."

"Amy," Paul called. "Will you come down to the kitchen for a minute please?"

Amy had heard pieces of the conversation. She shivered. It was that Lieutenant Sansone. Why did he have to call on Sunday? She wished Mom was here. She wouldn't let the trooper within a mile of the house. "I'm sort of busy right now," Amy answered.

"Please come down," Paul replied.

When Amy leaned against the sink, eyes on the floor, he said, "I've always been honest with you and Stephen, and until recently I had no reason to believe you weren't honest with me. Sometimes being honest, either with someone else, or even with yourself, is tough. I can understand that, but it doesn't make it all right. A boy has been killed. There is nothing more serious in society than murder. His life was taken from him, and the person who took that life must be punished. That is the law, Amy. I believe now that you were at the town beach with Donald Jenkins. So do the police."

Amy gasped. "It's not so. I tell you it's not so. You believe them, not me. That's not fair."

Paul paid no attention. "I can ask my lawyer to be present. He will stand between you and Sansone. He won't protect you altogether, but he will control the questioning. But he will also tell you what I am telling you now. You have to face up to what happened and what you know about it."

"I'll talk to him," Amy said softly. I won't admit anything,

131

she told herself, to the police or to Paul. If I say the same thing again and again, Sansone'll go away and leave me be, and then Paul will believe me, too. He's not my father. Dad wouldn't let Sansone keep after me, I know he wouldn't. Or would he? she wondered. She didn't try to answer that question.

During this visit Paul didn't ask Lieutenant Sansone to sit. The officer leaned against the broom cupboard, perfectly at ease, holding his hat, with two hands on the brim.

"I won't be long, Amy," he said with an attempted smile, a wolfish smile it seemed to the girl. "I'll come right to the point. Chief Torbert and I think you haven't told us some things you know."

Amy forced herself to stare at Sansone. She was silent.

"At your school you are sometimes called the princess?"

Paul spoke up. "Lieutenant. What kind of a question is that?"

"Please, Mr. Bruce. It is important. Well, Amy, is that true?"

"I can't say. Not to my face, anyway. Maybe behind my back." She was certain what the next question would be.

"Did no one ever call you Princess to your face—or on the telephone?"

"On the phone, yes, whoever it was. He told Milly, the operator, he wanted to speak to the princess. My friends knew that."

"And the Graveyard Gang thought maybe the caller was Donald Jenkins, because they knew that was what he called you."

Amy nodded. "But we weren't sure he was the caller."

"What do you think now?"

"About that?"

132

"Yes, about being the princess to Donald Jenkins."

"I haven't thought about it."

"It's important to us, Amy. You see, Mrs. Jenkins tells me Donald talked about his princess, although he didn't say who she was. And she remembers that Monday afternoon, that cold rainy afternoon, when she asked him why he was going swimming, he told her he was going to see the princess. Was that you, Amy?"

Amy put her head down. She couldn't face Lieutenant Sansone. "No," she murmured. "I didn't go to the beach on Monday."

"Where were you Monday afternoon?"

"She was here most of the afternoon," Paul said.

"Did you go out, Amy?" the officer persisted.

"Yes, down to Agatha's."

Paul looked at her sharply. He knows, Amy thought, that I'm lying. Agatha would back her up if she asked her to. Agatha was her friend. Maybe she wouldn't even remember that Amy wasn't there.

"I see," Sansone said. "Somehow, not from us, I want you and Mr. Bruce to understand, Mrs. Jenkins has it in her head that Amy Abbott is the princess, and that Amy Abbott was the one who killed her son, and Amy Abbott . . ."

"Lieutenant!" Paul commanded.

The officer paused. "You have told me, Amy, that you did go swimming every afternoon the week before that on hot days and cold days."

"Yes."

"And you were all by yourself. You met no one, you saw no one?"

"One afternoon, maybe Monday, there was a woman with two kids down at the beach end of the pond."

133

"Mrs. Schrader. She has told us she saw a girl and boy down by the graveyard path."

"It wasn't me," Amy said. "It might have been him, Donald, I mean, but it wasn't me. I dived in and swam out into the lake for a few minutes and came straight home. It could have been anyone. Other people use that path. Or maybe she saw me and thought I was with someone. It could happen, I guess. That part of the beach is in the shade late in the afternoon."

Lieutenant Sansone listened. He scratched an eyebrow. He looked at Paul Bruce, shrugged, and took a deep breath. He's through, Amy thought. Paul wasn't going to let him go on. She was safe. Lieutenant Sansone wouldn't be back.

"Who do you think could have killed Donald Jenkins, Amy?" Sansone asked. "What do they say at school? I need all the help I can get, because Torbert and I are stumped. Confidentially, we don't have the vaguest idea right now. Someone had a fight, we figure, with Donald Jenkins. The medical examiner tells us someone grabbed a rock, almost certainly there in the parking lot, and almost certainly hit him in the back of his head hard enough to fracture his skull, and then for good measure hit Donald Jenkins on top of the head and . . ."

"Lieutenant!" Paul shouted. "Out! Out of the house at once and don't come back. I forbid it."

Sansone put on his hat. "And," he continued coldly, "almost certainly that person dragged Donald to the pond and left him there to drown if he wasn't already dead and . . ."

"No," Amy screamed. "No, no, no." She ran from the kitchen. "No! I didn't. I didn't."

·30·

"We had better get your friends together to discuss the yard sale," Agatha said. "It's a warm afternoon. Why don't we use the grill Amy and I found in the cellar? I'll buy some charcoal while you call the gang."

"That's a good idea," Sandy said. "It's hard to get everyone together on a school day."

Malcolm Torbert was hunched over a cup of coffee at the counter in the general store. He did not look like a happy man.

Agatha did her shopping and put the basket on a stool and sat down next to the chief of police. "Bad day, Malcolm?"

Malcolm didn't answer. He shoved his cup across the counter to Mrs. Reed's daughter, who was home from college for the weekend. "A refill, Emily." He rubbed his hand over his craggy countenance. "What I don't understand is how in this little town, where it's everybody's business to keep track of everybody else's business, where a cat can't cross the road without being seen, someone went to the town beach, killed the Jenkins boy, and left. That road to the beach is right opposite Tom Martin's gas station. There were folks there, some of them talking outside, right up to closing time. No one saw a thing. Maybe Sansone is right, the Abbott girl took care of Donald. I don't see how she dragged him from the car to the water. Donald was a big boy. But you can never tell what people can do." Torbert lowered his voice as Emily put the coffee in front of him.

"You don't believe that, do you?" Agatha asked.

"I don't know what I believe. Sansone has me running around being useless. If I'd been there, the Abbott kid might have talked to *me* from the start."

"Sansone went back?"

"Yeah. She denied ever seeing the boy at the beach, denied being there Monday, broke down, and ran upstairs. Sansone has had his last crack at her. The next time her father will have a roomful of lawyers and psychologists. No one is going to shut Mrs. Jenkins up, either. She wants to hang the girl from the nearest light pole. It's a mess, Agatha."

"Maybe it *was* a crazy, a guy from anywhere in a car, who just happened to turn down to the pond, had a fight with the boy, and went on his way."

"That's what Sansone says, either that or the Abbott girl. There was this guy—or a woman, for all anybody knows— who was a serial killer. He knocked off five or six motorists at rest stops years ago. Pulled up next to their cars, leaned over and shot them, and drove off. Then he stopped. No one ever caught him."

"I remember," Agatha said.

"That's not what we have here," Malcolm said. "No gun, just a rock from the side of the lot where the road scraper pushed a million rocks when they leveled the lot. Car? No one saw a car going or coming. Martin was pumping gas all evening. He saw Donald's old heap go to the pond about four o'clock on Monday. He saw it go down there every day the week before and saw it come out. Nobody in the car with him, according to Tom. The boy usually waved. He didn't see it come back on Monday, didn't see a single car. Now isn't that strange?"

Agatha picked up the shopping basket. "I have to go, Malcolm. The Graveyard Gang is having a cookout this afternoon. Have you talked to them?"

"Sansone did. Deputy MacDonald and I were looking for a three-pound, blood-covered smooth rock in the parking lot," Torbert said bitterly. "We didn't find it."

"Come by for a hot dog at four-thirty on your way home," Agatha insisted. "One of the kids lives next door to the Jenkinses."

Torbert smiled at last. "Do you think I don't know where everyone in Wingate lives, Agatha?"

Agatha didn't answer. "Come on by," she said again as Mrs. Reed added up the purchases.

"That will be twelve dollars and two cents," Mrs. Reed said. "I don't have much change. You can owe me the two cents. Malcolm is taking it hard," she whispered. "I don't like that Sansone fellow. He's too smart for his own good."

"He's a good officer." Agatha felt obliged to stand up for a fellow police officer.

"He may be, but he doesn't know this town," Mrs. Reed said mysteriously.

The coals in the grill had lost their glow by the time Chief Torbert made an appearance. Only Amy Abbott, who, up to the moment of his arrival, had been talking to her friends, found his presence awkward. Amy withdrew, Agatha saw at once, lowering her head and hunching her shoulders forward as though expecting a blow. Agatha drew Malcolm inside

137

away from the girls. "Come talk with me for a while," she ordered. "Let Amy get used to you. Take the girls home in the cruiser afterward. The other kids know you, Amy doesn't."

When the late afternoon sun had almost disappeared, Agatha took the ice cream from the freezer. "We'll have dessert inside," she told Sandy. "Bring the girls in. Get Amy to help you."

"Now," she said when they were seated, "Chief Torbert will tell us what we must do for the yard sale. Do we need a permit, Malcolm?"

The chief shook his head. "Just keep the cars parked well off the road, that's about it. Close down before dark. It's getting that way now. I'll take you girls home when you're ready."

"We can walk," Wilma said. "It's not far."

"Agatha said I was to take you home. She's the boss."

"Can you tell us about Donald Jenkins?" Cathy spoke up. "I live next door. When I tell Mom and Dad how I got home, they'll want to know about Donald."

"So does everyone else," Malcolm said. "No comment, I guess. That means we don't know. But we'll find out, tell your folks that."

"My mother thinks that creepy Perry Whitman did it," Cathy went on.

"No comment."

"He's started coming by the Jenkins house again. He wasn't there all summer. Now he's back."

"Who's Perry Whitman?" Agatha asked innocently.

"Donald's friend," Sandy explained. "I told you about him."

"Oh, yes. I remember. The boy in the graveyard with Donald."

"Mom thinks they had a fight early in the summer, because we saw him at the Jenkinses every day before that. They came home together from the school bus. It's funny he's coming to see the Jenkinses with Donald gone, don't you think?"

Keep it going, Cathy, Agatha asked silently. "I don't know about that," she said. "It seems natural enough that he should want to console the family."

"Maybe," Cathy said, "but I sure wouldn't want Perry Whitman consoling me."

"Me, either," Wilma said. She stood up. "I'll take the ride now, Chief Torbert. My mother will be worrying soon. She's scared someone will kill me, too, I guess."

·31·

Sandy brought Amy to Agatha's house after soccer practice on Wednesday. "Amy's really good," she whispered as she took two cans of root beer from the refrigerator. "She's the fastest kid on the team, including the boys."

"How did school go?" Agatha asked.

"Not so good. Amy sits by herself in the back of the room. One of us sits next to her. We take turns. The kids keep looking at her and whispering. Amy can hear them. It's rough."

"Do you think she'd like to stay to supper?" Agatha asked.

"I'll see."

"You change," Agatha told her. "I'll ask."

Amy was standing at the door to the side porch. The long shadows from the graveyard trees stretched to the edge of the soccer field. "It's a beautiful time of year, isn't it?" Agatha said. "The view from your house across the river to the mountains must be extraordinary. Here's a root beer. Why don't you stay for supper? I'll drive you home afterward. Chipped beef on toast and a chunk of lettuce."

Amy spoke over her shoulder. "This is a neat place. I didn't realize how nice it was the week I was here. It gets lonely up where we live." Amy sighed. "It will be all right when I get older, I suppose, and can get around more. My brother says he's going to live there. He hasn't told Mom yet."

"How is your mother?" As soon as the words came out, Agatha realized she had made a mistake.

Amy was silent. She shook her head and turned to face Agatha. She is older than the others, Agatha understood again. Right now she could pass for eighteen. The Bigmouth business was wearing Amy down. The dark circles under her eyes were more pronounced. She was biting her lip. "Not too good," she brought herself to say. "She read about Donald Jenkins in the Boston paper and blew up at Paul and me on the phone. Her doctor said he'd see to it she didn't get any more papers for a while. She's going through a tough period of adjustment, he said."

"And you?" Agatha asked softly.

"I try not to think of her too much. I have my own problems, I guess you know."

"With Lieutenant Sansone?"

"Not just him. With Donald's mother—and with Paul."

"Sandy says you're a great soccer player. You can run like the wind, she told me."

"In the spring I used to run with Paul in the morning. We'd finish off with a sprint, just before we came to the driveway."

"I saw you last week leap over the graveyard wall like a deer and tear across the soccer field. At least, I think it was you."

Startled, Amy asked, "When?"

"Last Monday, late in the afternoon."

141

Amy paused. She took a deep breath. "It was me," she muttered. She might as well tell Agatha. Everyone else seemed to know by now.

Don't press, Agatha told herself. Let Amy talk at her own speed. "Well, I have to put the bread in the toaster."

Agatha spread the creamed chipped beef on the toast, placed a quarter head of lettuce next to it, and served the two girls. "How was school?" she asked, pulling her chair to the table.

Sandy glanced across the table and waited for Amy to answer. "Not too good," Amy explained. "Sort of like last year, only worse. You tell her, Sandy."

"You want me to?"

"Yes."

"The kids at school are talking about Amy and Donald Jenkins. They sort of look at her and turn away. I don't think they mean anything; the thing is they don't know what to do."

"That's not right, Sandy. You know what they're saying. Mrs. Jenkins is telling anyone who will listen that I killed her son. I want to scream that I didn't do any such thing, but I can't. I just want to crawl away where they can't see me."

Agatha didn't say a word. It was all coming out.

"Paul says I have to face up to it. Face up to what? That I ran into Bigmouth Jenkins at the beach and talked to him? What's wrong with that? We just sat and talked, and he took me home in his car. He was going away, you know. He told me. He didn't like Wingate people any better than my mother did. They made him feel like the village idiot just because he stayed back a couple of times. He wasn't stupid."

142

Amy's voice rose. "He was really intelligent about lots of things, not book things, other things like cars and wild animals, things like that." Amy wiped her eyes.

"It's all right, Amy," Sandy said. "Cathy told us he was a nice guy when you got to know him."

"He was, but I can't run around school saying he was a nice guy. I don't even know why his mother thinks I hit him. He was sitting there in his car when I left him."

"You told Lieutenant Sansone that?" asked Agatha.

Amy shook her head. "No. He thinks I killed Donald. I know he does."

"I don't believe that, Amy. He wants to find out what went on, that's all. He figures there's a chance you know something useful to the Chief and him."

"I can't talk to him," Amy said. "He looks at you with those hard eyes, trying to trap you. I can't talk to him. I won't. Paul will get a lawyer the next time, he said."

"How about to Malcolm Torbert?" Agatha asked.

"I don't know. Maybe."

"Would you try? With your friends, the Graveyard Gang, I have a feeling that all of you can help, that there's something you girls have seen or heard or thought about, something you've forgotten perhaps, that Torbert can use."

"That's a good idea," Sandy exclaimed. "Remember the evening Bigmouth made us jump in the ditch, Sandy? He was the one who laughed at us. The other guy, Perry Whitman, didn't laugh at us. He just stared. Like when we had our first meeting. Perry just stood behind Donald and stared. It made me feel funny. We'll all talk to the chief. It won't be only you, Amy."

"What do you think, Agatha?" Amy asked.

143

"He won't accuse you, Amy. Why don't you ask your stepfather? I'll take you home now, and we'll ask him."

Amy marched into the kitchen like a good soldier. "I was about to call," Paul greeted her. "It's not that late, but it's almost dark by six-thirty these days. How are you, Mrs. Bates?"

"I lied to you, Dad," Amy began abruptly. "I was at the lake with Donald Jenkins last Monday and the week before. And he brought me home in his old car," she said defiantly.

"I know that, Amy." Paul put his arm around his stepdaughter. "Even before Mrs. Bates said anything, I knew it. You were a different person that week. You weren't telling me what you were doing. Do you understand, it was the secret that told me? Not about Donald, of course, but that something was going on I wasn't supposed to know about."

"It was Mom at first," Amy confessed. "I don't want her to find out. Then it was everyone I couldn't talk to. They wouldn't have understood about Bigmouth."

"You were ashamed of him?" Paul asked.

"Yes."

"Why was that, Amy? He was your friend."

"He wasn't like us. Or like the other kids at school."

"No, I suppose he wasn't. But these things don't matter most of the time, do they, Mrs. Bates?"

Agatha shook her head. "I think Amy knows that. She wants to talk to Chief Torbert to set the matter straight. We think the Graveyard Gang can help, too. Tomorrow afternoon after school, perhaps. Right, Amy?"

"After soccer," Amy said.

"I'm going to shower and do my homework." She reached up to kiss Paul's cheek.

"And Lieutenant Sansone?" Paul asked Agatha.

"Malcolm can deal with him. We'll try to get him headed in another direction."

Paul held out his hand. "Thank you. You don't want me around tomorrow, correct?"

"Later, maybe. Just the Graveyard Gang tomorrow."

·32·

"You're certain you saw no one at the beach?" Malcolm Torbert asked again.

"No," Amy answered. "Just the woman and the two kids the first afternoon."

"Mrs. Schrader?"

"I guess," Amy said. "I couldn't see her all that well. Anyway, I don't know Mrs. Schrader."

"She saw you," Torbert said.

"Me, or a girl and a boy?" Amy asked.

Good for you, Amy. Don't let him get away with that, Agatha Bates thought. "Shame on you, Malcolm. You're behaving like Lieutenant Sansone."

"And you say Donald Jenkins drove you home?" Torbert went on.

"Not Monday," Amy said. "He asked, but I said no. And not the next Monday. I've told you that. And not Saturday or Sunday. We were taking my brother to school."

"But Tuesday, Wednesday, Thursday, and Friday, you rode those days with Donald in his car?"

"Yes, to the end of our driveway."

"Nowhere else?"

"Malcolm," Agatha warned. "That's out of bounds."

146

"All right, Agatha." The chief sighed. "Donald drove you from the pond parking lot out to the main road, down Main Street to Old Winthrop Road, directly to your place?"

"Yes. One of the days, maybe Tuesday, we drove down Sandy's lane. We stopped for a second and backed out to the road. That was it. I wanted to see if maybe Sandy's mother had come back or something."

Torbert pressed on. "I wonder how on those four days, Bill Martin saw Donald drive his car from the pond road onto the main road, a couple of times at least, but that was all he saw. Where were you, Amy?"

"I scrunched down in the front seat where no one could see me, until we came to Old Winthrop Road," Amy told Torbert.

"Afraid Mrs. Reed might see you?" Malcolm laughed.

"Anybody," Amy confessed. "I wasn't ashamed to be riding with Bigmouth. It was just . . ."

"It's all right," Wilma said. "If I was out in a car with a boy, you can bet I wouldn't want my mother to find out about it. I'd have been hiding in the trunk."

Everyone laughed. "Amy's mother has a thing about Wingate," Agatha explained. "It's common knowledge."

Chief Torbert paid her no attention. "So no one, apparently, except Mrs. Schrader, saw you two together, no one that you can recollect."

"I wasn't looking for people to see me," Amy said.

"But you stopped at Sandy's place? If Mrs. Prescott had been home, she would have seen Donald and you."

"I thought about that later. I felt pretty dumb."

"Nowhere else?" Torbert insisted.

Amy couldn't understand why it was so important whether someone had seen her riding in Donald's convertible. What

147

would that prove? She had already told the chief half a dozen times she was there. She tried to concentrate on each ride home. There was no way she could have seen anything until she'd sat up. She was absolutely certain they hadn't passed a car on Old Winthrop Road. She almost never met a car there. People took the paved road when they wanted to go to Winthrop. Amy passed the trip slowly through her memory. There was that tractor at the Whitman farm. It was always there, next to the fallen-down barn. Was it moving up the lane one day? She couldn't be sure. It wasn't parked at the top, next to the rusty mailbox on the tilted post. She would have remembered something like that. "Well," she began, and paused.

Torbert waited. "Well what, Amy?" he finally asked.

"Maybe—I can't be sure—there was someone on the Whitmans' tractor one afternoon. Maybe it was moving or parked on the lane with someone on it. I can't be sure. That's all I can remember."

"Perry or his father?"

Amy shook her head.

"And nothing or no one the Monday when you were running home."

"I didn't look. I had my head down," Amy said.

"And the person you saw, Agatha, it was Amy coming out of the graveyard."

"Amy told you it was her, Malcolm."

"Still, it's possible, isn't it, you missed Amy Abbott and saw someone else?"

"Another girl, yes. Another girl who looked and moved like Amy."

"Toward five o'clock, you said?" Torbert asked.

"Toward five. I can be definite about that," Agatha responded. "What did the coroner tell Lieutenant Sansone?"

"He didn't want to say exactly at first. He did a lot of tests. Donald might have died, he told Sansone this morning, later in the evening."

"You mean it probably *was* later in the evening. How much later?" Agatha demanded.

"He still can't be sure, Agatha. You know that half the time it's a guess. Especially in the water."

The Graveyard Gang was listening now, but Agatha didn't care. "How much later, Malcolm?" she asked firmly.

"A couple of hours, maybe."

So Sansone's playing games with Amy Abbott, Agatha thought. She wouldn't press the point further in front of the girls. She would catch Malcolm alone. It was time to shut Mrs. Jenkins up. She listened to Torbert questioning the girls.

"There's nothing you girls can tell me, no other 'princess' in the school? Anyone Donald used to fight with when he was at Bromfield? How about you, Cathy? Friends of Donald who came to visit, someone Mrs. Jenkins might have forgotten about?"

Cathy shook her head. "Only Perry Whitman, but they never fought that I know of. Perry followed Bigmouth around. Donald did all the talking, and Perry nodded with that sad smile. I guess they talked back and forth in the house. You can look into the Jenkins' kitchen from our house. They might have been talking at the kitchen table."

"But not this summer?" Torbert asked.

"They couldn't," Cathy explained. "Bigmouth workcd until real late at the gas station, evenings, and weekends, too."

"Yes, that's right," Chief Torbert agreed. "I'll report to

Sansone," he told Agatha. "I doubt he'll be back to see you for a while, Amy. Thanks for your help."

"I'll walk you to your car, Malcolm," Agatha said. Outside she turned to Torbert angrily. "What's Sansone up to, letting that Jenkins woman blab to everyone that Amy killed her boy? What was he doing driving her to a breakdown?"

"Keeping the pressure on her, Agatha. She was all we had. It was possible that Donald told her something about himself—a fight or something. And we didn't know the time until finally today from the coroner. He's told Mrs. Jenkins that Amy is in the clear. But the woman is upset, Agatha. Rich kid in town with a snooty mother. Her baby on the beach with his princess, not telling his mother about it. That won't go down easy with Mrs. Jenkins. I'll talk to her this time."

"You got something from the girls, didn't you, Malcolm?"

"We'll see, Agatha, we'll see."

·33·

"Mom says . . ." Cathy was talking when Agatha returned to the living room. She saw Agatha and hushed.

Was it girl talk, or was Cathy embarrassed? "I'm sorry I interrupted," Agatha said. "What did your mother say, Cathy?"

"Nothing much, just that . . . well, nothing, really. Afterward she said she shouldn't be talking that way."

"Pizza in fifteen minutes," Agatha said. "We'll eat in the kitchen. Bring an extra chair, Sandy."

What had Cathy's mother been saying that the girl didn't want to share with her? There was bound to be speculation in Wingate about Bigmouth's death. Amy Abbott must have been a useful scapegoat for town talk, Agatha supposed. In spite of herself, Agatha felt herself being drawn into the mystery. But now that Amy had explained herself, there was less reason than ever for her to concern herself. She smelled burning cheese. "Pizza," she called, and pulled open the oven door.

When Agatha had delivered the last of the Graveyard Gang, she returned slowly down Old Winthrop Road. She paused across from the lane to the Whitman farm. A light shone behind a single window, probably the kitchen. The house was a dark shadow in back of the lighted window. What went on there? Agatha wondered. A strange boy with a strange, if not even stranger, father. Did the creepy Perry Whitman have a mother? No one had mentioned her, if she existed. No one talked much about Perry except to say he was creepy. What would he do now that his only friend, Bigmouth Jenkins, was gone?

Right now, Sandy told her, he was spending a lot of time at the Jenkinses. This was information she had from Cathy. Mrs. Cameron paid a daily visit to the Jenkinses, usually with a casserole or a loaf of home-baked bread. In the evenings Perry and Mr. Jenkins were sitting at the kitchen table, just sitting, Cathy reported—not talking, just sitting, like Perry used to sit there with Donald. Her mother said it was creepier than ever.

"Why creepy? Didn't Perry used to eat supper there with the Jenkinses a lot?" Agatha asked.

Sandy couldn't answer. "Maybe it's because Perry has sort of taken Donald's place. Cathy says her mother has this thing about Perry. She wouldn't ever leave Cathy and her brother in the house alone, even to go down to the general store, when Perry was next door. Not once, Cathy says."

So that's what Cathy was telling the gang, Agatha thought. Kids were funny about things like that. Agatha couldn't decide whether Cathy had shut up to protect her mother or the Jenkinses. Was Mrs. Cameron being overprotective or did she have genuine fears about the boy? It didn't seem right that Perry Whitman was the town creep because of his father or because he wasn't loud and rude like some of the boys Agatha had seen goofing around at Martin's and the general store. Perry Whitman must have been the first person Malcolm Torbert thought of when he discovered Donald

Jenkins had been murdered. Apparently Perry had not turned out to be a good suspect, for some reason.

"Cathy's mother thinks Perry is telling the Jenkinses things about Amy. Last week one day when she went to visit she heard him say something about Amy the princess, but she couldn't hear what it was."

"That's not strange, Sandy. Apparently Donald as much as told his folks he was meeting Amy."

"I know, but Cathy's mother is convinced it was Perry who killed Donald. We're not supposed to say anything about that. Mr. Cameron told her she should keep her suspicions to herself, she didn't have a shred of evidence to be talking that way."

"I see," Agatha said. "Cathy's father is right. Gossip has a way of hurting people. Look at poor Amy. Does Mrs. Cameron have any good reasons, beyond the fact Perry is a creep?"

"No. That's what Cathy was telling us when you came back inside. But she thinks she knows how he could have gone to the beach. It's a Graveyard Gang secret. I guess I shouldn't be telling you."

"I don't want to hear it if it's really and truly a secret," Agatha said.

"Cathy's probably exaggerating. It can't be much of a secret. Well, what Cathy's mother said was that maybe, just maybe, Perry Whitman came through the woods at the bottom of his pasture and across the marsh to the lake. Her mother, Cathy's grandmother, once told Cathy's mother that the Whitman farm used to go right down to the edge of the lake. When she was a girl they used to go on picnics there or something. Then the Whitmans sold their cows and the pasture grew up and the lake filled in back there, and now

153

that part of the lake, the good part, only reaches to down in back of the graveyard."

Agatha calculated, "That must have been sixty years ago or so."

"I guess. Cathy doesn't know."

"What does Mrs. Cameron think went on?" Agatha asked. "That Perry Whitman slipped down through the woods and across the marsh and sneaked up on his friend and killed him? That does seem remote, I must say."

"Cathy's father thought the same thing. The motive, he asked his wife, what was the motive? You have to have a motive. Mrs. Cameron didn't have one. Anyway, it's a secret, so don't tell anyone, not even Chief Torbert."

"Not a word will pass these lips," Agatha promised. But the thoughts remained after Sandy went to her room. Possibly, just possibly, it hadn't occurred to Torbert, or Lieutenant Sansone, that Perry Whitman didn't have to walk down Main Street. Tomorrow, Agatha promised herself, she would take a look at that end of the town pond.

Still, Torbert and Sansone weren't fools. Perry Whitman must have been home with his dad Monday evening. And even if he wasn't, what possible reason did he have to hurt Donald Jenkins? Agatha could hear Cathy's mother saying to her husband, "Because the boy is crazy. Isn't that reason enough?"

Even crazy people have reasons, Agatha knew. Crazy reasons, maybe, but reasons.

·34·

Amid all the junk in the cellar Henry had *not,* Agatha discovered, squirreled away a pair of rubber boots. He hadn't even worn leather boots on the winter weekends in Wingate, Agatha now recalled, just the disgusting sneakers he was so partial to in every season. "My country shoes," he used to call them. But Arthur Harper next-door did have boots, trim, gray, red-soled rubber boots that came up to his knees.

"You're not wearing your boots this morning, are you, Arthur?" she asked when Arthur came to the door.

"Those are my spring gardening boots, Agatha, as you should know by now. They will be too big for you. Come on in. I'll bring them up from the cellar. You've had a lot of visitors the last couple of days," Arthur commented, handing Agatha the boots. "You might want to stuff some paper towels in the toe to keep them from sliding off your feet. I noticed Chief Torbert a couple of times. Are you looking into the Jenkins boy's murder?"

Agatha shook her head. "Malcolm wanted to talk to some of Sandy's friends about the boy's friends and such."

"Mrs. Reed said Mrs. Jenkins was telling everyone who would listen that some girl named Abbott had hit the boy with a rock. The Abbotts are the rich, new family up on Old

Winthrop Road, aren't they? Anything to it, do you think? Mrs. Reed said—"

"That Amy was at my place for a few days, is that it, Arthur?"

"Sort of."

Agatha took the boots and turned to leave. "Tell Mrs. Reed that Amy was helping clean out my cellar, not burying a body there. Thanks for the boots. I'll bring them back this afternoon."

Agatha gathered what she reckoned she needed for the expedition—boots, gloves, nylon jacket, heavy pants, two or three pairs of socks, and something for the hair, a bandanna, maybe. Most likely there would be patches of brambles, wild roses, or blackberries along the way. They could be fierce.

Not more than several hundred yards after she'd turned left along the edge of the pond, Agatha came to a clutter of dead trees and stumps and a scraggle of bushes, alders, and swamp maples. The water was clogged with grass and reeds. Staying as close as she could to the back of the pond, Agatha pushed her way through the underbrush.

To her right the marsh led to woods. Beyond must be the Jenkinses' pasture, Agatha thought. She moved into the marsh. The third step plunged her feet through mud. Water poured over the tops of Arthur's boots. Step by step Agatha picked her way through the swamp. Gradually the footing became firmer, until she came to the grove of oak and evergreens.

Leaning against a tree, she emptied the boots one at a time. She pulled out the wads of wet towels. Boots flopping, she set out in the direction she guessed the Whitman farm lay. After ten minutes she came to the tree line. Beyond,

156

an overgrown field stretched to the Whitmans' tumbledown barn and house. It was not more than a hundred and fifty yards from where she stood. Some of the panes in the windows facing the woods were broken. At the back of the barn was abandoned farm equipment, an ancient truck, and the remains of a rusty tractor. A trail of smoke rose from the chimney of the house.

Agatha heard a door slam. She stepped back into the trees. A bent-over man in overalls picked up an armload of wood from the woodpile. He disappeared into the house. Agatha looked at her watch: 10:25. She turned back toward the lake. When she reached the town beach, she looked at her watch again: 11:03.

Take away five minutes from Perry Whitman for knowing the way, add she could only guess how many minutes for a discussion with Donald, plus another half an hour to return to the farm, and it came to something over an hour, probably a good deal more.

What was she trying to find out, anyway? Agatha asked herself. Either Perry Whitman came this way and his father hadn't been paying attention to where his son was, or Perry had gone down Main Street without being seen. Either way, he could have killed Donald Jenkins. Still, it was interesting that Perry Whitman had a way of getting to the beach without being seen.

As she came out of the graveyard and onto the soccer field, Agatha saw a figure sitting on her side porch. She squinted. It was Malcolm. She lifted a hand to greet him.

"I made it to be something over an hour," were Torbert's first words. "How about you?"

Agatha sat on the edge of the porch to dump the muddy water from the boots. She spread three pairs of socks over the edge of a rocker and unzipped her jacket. "I'd say closer to an hour and a half. They must have had a talk before the fight or whatever happened, don't you think?"

"I'm not sure. Maybe Perry just came up with a rock and hit Donald when he wasn't looking."

"After he saw Amy in the front seat of Donald's car, the boy must have waited out of sight at the top of the lane every afternoon to keep track of them."

Malcolm nodded. "It's possible. Monday, when he saw Amy run by, he decided to see if Donald was at the beach. He must have had something in mind if he went the back way."

"He wanted to know if Amy was Donald's new friend," Agatha mused.

"Something like that, maybe," Malcolm agreed.

"It's a hard way to get to the beach," Agatha said.

"About fifteen to eighteen minutes from his farm to the beach, if you take the road. You reckon Perry was angry or hurt or confused or betrayed or whatever, and he didn't want to see anyone along the way?"

"What did his father say?" Agatha asked.

"Sansone talked to him first off. Said the boy was watching television with him."

"You don't think it's remotely possible Perry's father did it?"

"Naw, the old man is crippled up with arthritis. Perry does most of the farm work, such as it is."

"What did Sansone say?" Agatha asked.

"He liked the Amy Abbott scenario. Donald made a pass at a high-strung girl who just wanted to be friendly, and she went over the edge."

"What's he say now?"

158

"He's come around to consider Perry Whitman. If the old man sticks to his story, it's going to be hard to prove."

"What are you going to do, Malcolm?"

"Ask you to make a pot of coffee. I'll clean out Arthur's boots with the garden hose here."

"After that, Chief Torbert?" Agatha insisted.

"Wait. Sansone and I decided we'd wait awhile."

"Perry is trying to replace Donald at the Jenkins house, isn't he?"

"That's what we figure, you and Sansone and I, at least. I haven't checked with Mary Reed. There's no sense in pushing. Perry isn't going anywhere. Sooner or later he'll let it all out."

·35·

"Where's Amy?" Sandy asked. She and Cathy sat on Wilma's bed, waiting for Wilma to return with a plate of brownies.

"This is a special meeting of the club," Cathy replied. "Wilma and I agreed that Amy shouldn't be here, since we might be talking about her."

"What's the difference? Everyone else is, too. It's awful. Even after Miss Wilder made the speech, it didn't make any difference," Sandy said bitterly.

Only that morning Miss Wilder had started the day not by reading a poem but by telling the class that Chief Torbert had assured Mr. LaGrange that no one, repeat *no one,* in the Bromfield School was under suspicion for anything. That hadn't made any difference. Even while Miss Wilder was telling them, most of the class was looking around at Amy as if she was a Halloween madman, and at recess they clutched into groups of two and three to whisper about what their parents had said about what Donald's mother was telling anyone who would listen.

Wilma came back with the brownies. She closed the door tightly. She lowered her voice. "Talk softly. My mother thinks something strange is going on."

160

"Well, we can meet at my place next time," Cathy said. "I'll need a day or two to persuade Mom and my brother to leave us be. Or maybe we can meet at Agatha's. Could you ask, Sandy?"

"First, why don't you tell me what's going on."

"Cathy and I had this crazy idea," Wilma explained. "We talked it over after practice and decided to call you, but not Amy."

"The kids aren't going to let up on Amy," Cathy explained. "At least not until they find the actual killer. Last year Amy was the rich kid, this year she's the rich kid who dated the town delinquent and killed him. My mother says it's disgusting, and she's ready to leave town. She says the real murderer is walking around town free, spending most of his time next door, painting Donald's old car, which the Jenkinses gave him. It's sick."

Sandy hadn't heard about the car. "You mean Perry has the car now?"

"Yes. Mrs. Jenkins told Mom that Donald would have wanted his friend Perry Whitman to have it. It didn't make any difference to her that Donald hadn't even talked to Perry all summer for some reason. Then Mrs. Jenkins went into her speech about how corrupt the police are and wouldn't arrest the Abbott girl because her father was so rich. She's shut up a little bit, I guess, because Chief Torbert told her she'd be in trouble if she kept on. Mrs. Reed doesn't listen to her anymore and she, Mrs. Jenkins I mean, won't shop at her general store. Perry says he'll drive her over to the mall to do the shopping when he gets his license."

"That's really sick," Sandy agreed. "But why are we here?"

"Cathy and I decided to do something," Wilma continued.

161

"First, we want to know if Agatha has said anything to you about the murder. She's a police officer, she ought to have an idea."

"Not much," Sandy reported. "Mostly we talk about the yard sale. I don't feel right talking about Amy behind her back. I did ask Agatha last night about what your mother said, Cathy. Agatha said she might be right, and Torbert and Sansone would find out if it was so."

"See, I told you Mom was right, Wilma," Cathy said triumphantly. "Even my dad is starting to agree with her."

"Could you *please* tell me why we are here," Sandy asked again. "I have a lot of homework. I'm not as smart as you two."

"We had this idea. Wilma did actually," Cathy said. "Wilma has a nasty mind."

"Cathy!" Wilma protested. "Not half as nasty as yours and your mother's. You're the ones who started me thinking."

"Thinking about what? I'm dying of suspense." Sandy looked at her watch. It was almost dark outside. The wind had picked up, and the shutters on Wilma's little house were rattling.

"It's about Perry Whitman," Wilma said. "Remember those creepy phone calls last summer? I don't think Big-mouth made them. I think it was Perry Whitman. I explained to Cathy, and she agrees."

"What makes you think it was him? I never heard him say a word," Sandy declared.

"Well, Donald was pumping gas over in Coldstream. I figured he was busy pumping gas all the time and whatever else he did. He would have had to make the calls on a pay phone, maybe, or use the station phone and Sam, or what-

162

ever his name is, would have been on him. At the lodge they had to go find Amy to come to the phone every time, remember, and it took five minutes or so. Also, creepy phone calls don't sound like Bigmouth to me. Cathy agrees. He liked to talk and make a big show of things. It had to be Perry."

"Someone else could have," Sandy said.

"Not really. The voice wanted the princess. That's what Donald called Amy."

"You're right," Sandy said. What Wilma said made a lot of sense. "But why?"

"My mother," Cathy took up the discussion, "says creepy Perry was jealous. Donald got a job and left him behind. She didn't think of the phone calls, but Wilma and I did. Perry wanted to imitate Bigmouth and get to be his friend again. That's what kids do, you know."

"I guess you're right," Sandy agreed. "Especially if you're a little crazy. But it's no reason to kill someone."

"It is if your best friend trades you in for a rich kid. I've seen television shows where that happens. Haven't you, Wilma?" Cathy asked.

"I don't watch much," Wilma said. "I like to read."

"What do you want me to do, tell Agatha about your idea?" Sandy asked.

"No," Cathy said. "We have a better idea. It's not ours really, it was Perry Whitman's."

"Phone calls," Wilma interrupted. "Creepy phone calls— and notes in the mail."

"Scary, anonymous phone calls? I think that's against the law," Sandy said.

"Not anonymous, silly," Cathy said. "Phone calls and letters from Donald Jenkins."

Sandy was stunned. She tried to think about it. She reached out to take the last brownie before Cathy grabbed it.

"What do you think, Sandy?" Wilma asked. "We won't do it unless you agree. It's a Graveyard Gang project."

"I don't know. It's a great idea. I guess it might work. If Perry was crazy enough to kill his only friend, he just might believe you." The more she turned the plan over in her mind, the more Sandy was convinced that Cathy and Wilma were right. "You really think this will work?" she inquired.

Cathy and Wilma nodded.

"How?"

"Make him confess or something. We're not sure," Wilma said.

"What we need," Cathy explained, "is a person to call Perry in the middle of the night. Wilma and I can't."

"And a typewriter," Wilma added. "That old typewriter you said Agatha is putting out at the yard sale. Cathy and I don't have one—a computer, either. We don't want to try to use the ones at the school or the library. A typewriter, we decided, not a computer. An old typewriter with creepy keys and letters you can hardly read."

"Will you do it, Sandy?" Cathy asked. "It's for Amy. We're the four musketeers, remember?"

"I'm in," Sandy replied. She crossed her fingers and tapped Wilma's desk. "Knock on wood, the Graveyard Gang, through thick and thin."

·36·

Something was going on. Amy felt more alone than ever. Now it wasn't only the kids in the eighth-grade room who ignored her or glared at her if she came too close. She was used to them. But now it was Cathy and Wilma and even Sandy. One or another of them still sat next to her in the back row of the room, and they still ate together under the maple tree, where they were as friendly as ever; but you didn't have to be too sensitive to know that something was going on with them too.

Right after soccer practice, all three ran off to Wilma's or Cathy's house, calling, "See you tomorrow" over their shoulders. What was so important they wouldn't share with her? The Graveyard Gang was supposed to be arranging the yard sale, although Agatha still hadn't selected a date. There were signs to be made, prices to be affixed to sale items, decisions to be made on who would make the brownies and stuff.

It's time to get out of Wingate, she told herself, as she walked home after school. Even Agatha, who had been so friendly a couple of weeks ago, was never on the side porch after soccer to invite her in for a chat. It was like they had all gotten her to confess to Chief Torbert and right after that had forgotten about her. Or maybe, she suddenly thought,

165

they're ashamed because I'd been Bigmouth's friend. "I don't need them," she muttered. "I got along without them before all this happened, and I can get along without them now."

One good thing: She and Paul were closer than they had ever been. Every morning a little after six, he tapped on her door. "Running this morning, Amy?" She would struggle out of bed, splash water on her face, pull on her sweatshirt and sweatpants, and join Paul in the kitchen. They ran three miles, to the old mill and back. Amy showered and got ready for school while Paul set out the breakfast. Then Paul walked with her as far as the Prescotts'.

It was a routine that Amy slipped into without protest. She discovered that she could talk to Paul, in ways she never had done before, about Mom, about the strange behavior of the other musketeers, even about her father. She didn't need the club, she could take care of herself without the three of them, she told him. To her surprise, Paul disagreed. "That's wrong, Amy. You need friends to get through life. I've only begun to find that out for myself. It's not enough to sit in front of a computer all day looking after someone else's money. This summer I realized what a difference Stephen made. I hadn't worked with anyone since your father died. I was left almost as alone as your mom and you two children. What I think I'm saying"—Paul reached out to take Amy's hand—"is that I'm part of something again, and it feels good."

"I still don't know what's going on," Amy repeated. "All of a sudden, we stopped being together after school. They're together, I'm pretty sure, but *I'm* not. I was counting on them. That's why I want to move, maybe closer to Mom."

Paul waited a long time before he replied. When Crutch

put his head in Paul's lap to tell him please to put his plate on the floor for him to lick clean, Paul scratched the old dog and scraped Amy's scraps onto his own plate before he gave it to Crutch. "I don't know what's going to happen with Mom," he said. "Dr. Farber says he has noticed improvement, but she is a good way from coming home. I don't have to live here, Amy. We can live pretty much where we decide. But I still don't like the notion we're running away. Next year you'll be going to high school. If things keep on the way they are now, I promise you we'll leave Wingate. Let's wait and see. In the meantime, you have a soccer game tomorrow. Do you want to run in the morning?"

"Maybe I better not," Amy said. "Are you coming to the game?"

"I wouldn't miss it."

In the last minute of the game, Amy took a pass from Brad McKinnon, flashed between two Coldstream defenders, and pounded the ball past the diving goalie for the only score of the game. Screaming, the Wingate team piled on top of Amy.

"We didn't expect to win this one," Miss Wilder said to Paul on the sidelines. "Amy is a really great player."

"I'll take the gang in for cocoa and some gingerbread," Agatha said. "It turned out better than the cake I made a couple of weeks ago. Why don't you come along, Paul?"

"I'd love to," Paul accepted.

"Sandy," Agatha called, "bring Wilma and Cathy along with Amy for cocoa if they have time."

"I don't know," Sandy said. "I'll try."

Wilma and Cathy shook their heads impatiently. Agatha heard one of them say, "We can't, we just can't. Not *now*."

"Sorry, Agatha," Sandy called back. "We have something

167

to do. She hugged Amy. "You won it for us. We're not much of a team without you. See you tomorrow." She took off after Wilma and Cathy toward Main Street.

Agatha frowned. "I'd like to know what's going on. Every afternoon this week, Sandy goes off with those other two. Do you know what's up, Amy?"

"Nope," Amy replied bravely. "They haven't told me. Maybe it's about the yard sale."

"Nonsense," Agatha said. "We haven't even picked out a date. The leaves can't make up their minds when to turn. No, the three of them are up to something. This seems to have made an outcast of you, Amy. Don't let it bother you." Agatha smiled at Amy, who could not disguise her hurt.

She didn't answer. More than before she felt absolutely left out, this time in front of the team and Agatha and Paul, she realized. They made it easier for the other kids to ignore her. This time next year, she told herself, she would be long gone from the Bromfield School in Wingate, New Hampshire.

"And the typewriter," she heard Agatha speaking to Paul. "A ratty old portable Sarah brought home from college years ago. It ended up in the basement to collect mold and rust. Amy put it in the "to sell" pile, didn't you, Amy?"

"It worked all right," Amy said, "but the ribbon was rotten and some of the keys stuck. I don't think you'll get much for it."

"Nobody uses them anymore, Sandy informed me, but she dragged it into her room. I hear her using it, though I haven't the vaguest idea what for."

"Something for the yard sale, I bet," Amy said. "We were going to put announcements on the poles along Main Street. I think a Magic Marker would be better."

"You're right," Agatha said. "I think it was a letter or note or something. And the telephone, I forgot about that. Sandy wasn't calling you about three o'clock the other morning?"

"Not me," Amy said.

"Me, either." Paul laughed. "It's time for us to leave, Amy. My night for supper."

"It certainly was strange," Agatha Bates mused. "Wilma or Cathy, maybe, but I'm pretty sure Sandy didn't say anything. I heard the little ring my old phone always makes when you start to dial. That's what woke me up, halfway at least, and I listened to hear what was going on. Not a sound. Then Sandy went back to her room. No one answered, I guess. Or . . ." Agatha paused.

Amy and Paul, at the door, waited for Agatha to continue. "Well, it was nice to have you both drop by. Another home game next week, Sandy tells me. I'll be there to cheer you on, Amy."

·37·

Agatha heard the brief tinkle of the phone. Without opening her eyes, she turned on her side, telling herself she really must get the phone fixed. She raised one sleepy eyelid to glance at the bedside clock. 2:55. She was instantly awake. What was Sandy up to? She poked her feet into slippers and went into the hall. Sandy's door was half open. Agatha moved quietly toward the kitchen. The door was closed, a rim of light shining at the bottom. She heard a ghostly whisper. "Why did you do it? Why did you do it?"

The phone was put down. The light was turned off. The kitchen door opened. Sandy bumped into a figure standing beyond the door. She shrieked.

"I'm sorry, Sandy," Agatha apologized. "I heard a noise in the kitchen."

"Gee, you frightened me. I woke you up. I'm really sorry."

"It's awfully late—or early, I'm not sure which," Agatha commented.

"I'm sorry," Sandy repeated. Nothing more, only, "I'm sorry."

"Do you think it will work?" Agatha asked.

"You heard?"

Agatha turned on the light in back of the sofa. "Yes," she responded. "Will it work?"

"We hope so," Sandy said.

"How long have you been at it?"

"Let's see," Sandy counted. "Letter, phone, letter, phone, letter, letter, phone—that's this one, and tomorrow, a letter. Eight days, altogether."

"What do you expect to happen?" Agatha asked.

"We hope we'll upset Perry enough he'll confess or do something crazy. We aren't sure. Cathy's mother—she's at the Jenkins house every day, usually taking supper over—says Perry's acting strange, twitching and rolling his head around. He's saying funny things about Donald and himself, what they used to do together and what they had planned to do. And a lot of lies about Amy Abbott, things like, "I'm going to tell Chief Torbert about her," and so on."

"This is a dangerous game, Sandy. I don't need to tell you that."

"It's not a game, Agatha," Sandy protested. "We mean it. Amy won't have a chance in school, or in town, either, until they find the person who killed Donald Jenkins. All the Graveyard Gang is convinced Perry Whitman did it. Mrs. Cameron is certain. And you are, too, aren't you, Agatha? I sort of let Cathy and Wilma think that you were. Was I wrong?"

Good lord, Agatha thought. Did I let my suspicions become that obvious? "There's no evidence against Perry Whitman, Chief Torbert said."

"Maybe not yet, but Perry did it. We know he did. He went down to the bottom of his pasture and through the woods and marsh, where no one saw him. The two of them had a fight."

"If he went the back way," Agatha pointed out, "he must have had something wicked in mind to start with."

"Yes," Sandy agreed. "We think he did."

Agatha sighed. Apparently she had slept through the first phone call Sandy had made to the Whitmans. "So what is the gang doing?"

"Well, every other day, or once, two days in a row, we send Perry a note with a single question. Cathy and Wilma are in charge of the letters. They tell me what to type, and they mail the letters. We decided what to do on the phone. The first time I waited a few seconds after Perry answered and hung up. The next time I breathed heavy and moaned like a ghost. Tonight you heard what I said."

"And the letters?"

"The first one, 'Why?' The next one, 'Someone saw you.' Then, 'You better tell them.' Four, 'Why did you take my car?' And tomorrow, 'Tell my folks, Perry. They need to know.' We sign them all 'Donald.' "

"Do Mrs. Cameron and Mrs. Hughes know about this?" Agatha asked.

Sandy shook her head. "That's why I make the phone calls. Cathy and Wilma are afraid they'll get caught."

"And what about you, Sandy?" Agatha asked severely. "You are on the edge of breaking the law, if you haven't already broken it. Remember how upset Amy was when she got those crazy calls at the inn."

"We thought about that, Agatha," Sandy argued. "We've kept Amy out of this from the beginning. It was those phone calls that decided us. It was Perry Whitman on the phone this summer, not Bigmouth. It had to be him. He wanted to

172

do something to impress Donald, so he teased the princess the same way Bigmouth did."

That was pretty shrewd of the Graveyard Gang. "But it didn't work, you figured. They didn't renew their friendship."

"We don't know. Wilma says that Bigmouth was secretly fond of Amy, and he got mad at Perry when he found out about the calls and wouldn't have anything more to do with him. That's why he's telling the Jenkinses that Amy Abbott took Donald away from him."

So that was it, Agatha thought. Donald was the princess's lonely admirer, Perry Whitman the forgotten friend. The Graveyard Gang was swimming in dangerous waters. "Now what will you do?" she asked.

"We're going to wait to see what happens. I'm sorry I woke you up and used your phone without asking. I shouldn't have done that. But I couldn't slip out to the pay phone at the general store at three o'clock at night. We're scared, anyway, that Perry Whitman will figure out who's doing this."

"Unless he believes it's Donald, right?"

"If he was crazy enough to kill his best friend, he might be crazy enough to think Donald is in touch with him. Unless he figures out Donald didn't have a typewriter and couldn't type, either."

"And Amy?" Agatha reminded Sandy.

"We didn't want to get her into trouble. It didn't seem fair to us," Sandy explained.

"If Perry Whitman gives the letters and phone calls any serious thought, who do you suppose he will think is responsible? Who does Perry have on his mind?" Agatha wanted to know.

Startled, Sandy put her hand across her mouth. "Amy Abbott," she blurted. "We better tell her quick."

"I'll talk to Malcolm first thing in the morning—and her stepfather. You and your friends stay close to her. Why don't you have a meeting of the Graveyard Gang at Cathy's house after soccer. Paul or I will pick her up there. Now, let's go to bed, the both of us."

·38·

"We haven't had a meeting in a good while," Amy remarked to Sandy. "I thought the club had died." She hoped Sandy would tell her what had been going on with Wilma and Cathy the last couple of weeks.

Sandy avoided the suggestion. "Agatha finally set a date for the yard sale, next weekend. It's time for us to work out the details."

So the yard sale hadn't been what they were discussing. Amy felt relief that she hadn't been left out of that. "Don't worry," Paul had said, "you're not being left out. Those girls have other responsibilities, you must understand, which they don't share with everyone." Amy hadn't asked, "Like what?" Now Wilma and Cathy and Sandy and she were together again. That was all she wanted.

Wilma and Cathy were talking in a low voice ahead of them. Cathy said something that made Wilma wave her arms excitedly in the air. She looked around at Amy and smiled. "Did you walk to school this morning?" she asked.

Amy shook her head. The minute they came back from running, the phone had rung. Paul had listened, said, "I understand," and hung up. At the breakfast table, he told her he had to go to the general store and would take her to

175

school. Now Wilma was asking her how she got to school. What difference does it make? Amy wondered. She felt uneasy.

Cathy was in charge of the meeting, because it was at her house. "First, what about the notices? Black markers on colored construction paper?"

No one disapproved. "Good," Cathy said. "And a couple of big ones to put on the trees in front of Agatha's house. That ought to do it. Next, what about food? We can put the money we make in the treasury, right, Wilma?"

"Except what we borrow to buy stuff with: cider, hot dogs, rolls. My mother is making two cakes, free. Your mother promised to make doughnuts."

"Agatha and I are going to the market in the mall next week," Sandy said. "Things are cheaper there. She'll advance us the money."

"Don't buy cider. Dad has a friend who makes his own cider. We won't have to pay for that," Cathy said.

There was a knock at the door. Mrs. Cameron came in with four mugs of cocoa. "It's real cocoa," she said, "not that packaged stuff. Marshmallows in the cupboard if anyone wants them. I'll be right back. I'm going over to the Jenkinses for a minute. Perry is in the garage. I think they may have finished with the car. Your father called from Henderson, Cathy. He'll be home late."

Amy looked at Cathy. "What car?"

"You didn't know? It's Donald's. The Jenkinses gave it to Perry. They have been painting it all week. Now, let me see the list. Wilma has a waffle iron, almost new, a set of nesting tables, some good winter clothes, and some stuff her father left behind."

"Cathy!" Wilma protested.

176

"Well, he did, didn't he?" Cathy said. "Don't be so sensitive. We won't tell anyone whose they were. Mom has a lot of stuff, but I don't have the list yet. How about you, Amy?"

"Dad has told Agatha what he's delivering, a couple of cars' worth, he said. Some really old things, antiques, maybe."

"I'm calling Mom on Sunday," Sandy said. "She'll tell me what I can take from the house. It won't be much. We didn't have room for much of anything."

"These people will come by next Saturday," Cathy said. "The Gibsons, the O'Mearas, and Mrs. Harshburger. They'll put their own prices on. Oh, Mr. LaGrange will leave some old school furniture from the basement. Not on commission, he says. The money goes to the school athletic fund. That's it for today. Now, who wants to see the pictures of our trip to Boston? Mom just got them back."

They must have spent an hour looking at photographs. After she passed the last one to Wilma, Amy looked out the window. It was completely dark. She grabbed her jacket and book bag. "See you tomorrow," she said, and ran from the room.

"Wait!" Sandy shouted after her. "Phone your father or Agatha."

"It's okay," Amy called. "I carry a flashlight in my bag."

"It's all right," Cathy said. "Perry's next door." She gathered up the mugs. As she put them in the sink, her mother hurried into the kitchen.

"You'll never believe this," she exclaimed excitedly. "I'm still shaking. Give me the phone, Cathy. Have your friends left?"

Sandy and Wilma came into the kitchen, ready to leave.

"There you are," Mrs. Cameron said. "Let me tell you before I call Chief Torbert."

"Tell us what?" Cathy asked. "You're as pale as a ghost."

Her mother paid no attention. "I took a beef casserole to the Jenkinses. Mr. and Mrs. Jenkins were sitting at the kitchen table with a funny look on their faces. They didn't say anything. I put the casserole down and started to leave. Sometimes they don't talk; I'm used to it. But Mrs. Jenkins finally said—I could hardly hear her—'Nancy, could you do something for us? I don't think we can do it.'

"I said sure, and Mrs. Jenkins started to cry and came right out and said that Perry Whitman had told them he had had a fight with Donald at the beach and killed him. They were fighting over the Abbott girl and Donald's going away and Perry lost control. There was some more I don't have time to go into. Perry said Donald told him to confess. I told you he was crazy.

"Perry was like a son to them, Mrs. Jenkins said, and they couldn't bring themselves to call the police. It would be like turning Donald in. Someone had to do it, and they wanted me to call the station and tell the chief or his deputy, whoever answered."

"Where's Perry?" Sandy demanded.

"At his place, Mrs. Jenkins thinks. After he told them, he went out to the garage and drove away in the car they had painted. Give me the phone now, Cathy. Oh, here it is in my lap."

Sandy tore open the kitchen door and bounded down the steps. She was running full-steam before she hit the sidewalk. She could catch up to Amy by the time Mrs. Cameron told Malcolm Torbert the whole story. Main Street was empty, except for some people in front of the general store. Amy wasn't one of them. Breathing hard, Sandy raced toward Old Winthrop Road.

Half a mile ahead of her, Amy jogged along the road. As she came to the Whitmans' lane, she put her head down and sprinted. From the corner of her eye, she saw the shadow of a car parked near the top of the lane. Amy moved across the road, to face traffic, remembering again Bigmouth's warning. Amy felt a sense of terror. She reached in her bag for the flashlight.

The headlights picked up Amy as she passed the Prescotts' mailbox. Amy stepped well off the road, on the other side of the ditch, and waited. She clicked on the flashlight and held it toward the road in front of her. A car roared by, music blaring, a big green car that disappeared over the crest of the hill.

Amy breathed a sigh of relief. Why had she been so scared? she asked herself. It was silly. Holding the flashlight, she resumed her jogging.

Ahead of her there was a minute of silence, which was broken by the roar of a car motor. Distant lights cut high into the trees, flattened out at the top of the hill, and bore down on her. Amy backed into the ditch. She waved the flashlight. Petrified, she recognized Donald's old convertible headed toward her. It seemed to turn into another green car down a shady city street. Her legs refused to move. Paralyzed, she faced the rushing convertible. The flashlight slipped from her open fingers as she waited without a thought for the car to run over her.

With a fearful snarl of tires pulling at the ground, the car abruptly slashed toward the middle of the road. It turned over once, two times, three times, rolling away from Amy Abbott. The car's lights disappeared in a shower of glass. It turned over once more, smashing into the trunk of a roadside maple. A door ripped open and a figure was flung into the air as Donald's old car bounced from the tree onto the road, rolling over one last time.

Blue and white lights headed toward her. A siren wailed. Amy stepped from the ditch as the police cruiser braked. Chief Torbert walked in front of the police car to bend over the figure on the road. He returned to the cruiser. Amy could hear him speaking into his radio.

A figure ran past the chief's car, paused for a second at the accident, and hugged Amy. "Are you all right, Amy?" Sandy asked her urgently.

Amy shuddered. "I guess so. I thought—I thought for a second, it—it seemed like Dad's convertible and I—"

"It's all right now, Amy," Chief Torbert said. He had come up beside Amy.

"Is it Perry?" Amy asked.

"Yeah. It's Perry Whitman."

"Is he . . . ?"

"I can't say. It doesn't look good. I've called the ambulance. He tried to run you down, did he?"

"Yes, but he turned away, and the car went over and over."

Chief Torbert turned his flashlight on the brake marks gouged into the dirt. "It looks that way, doesn't it? He turned too sharp, I reckon, and the old car wouldn't make it."

From a distance wailed another siren. Chief Torbert headed back toward the wreck.

Sandy put her arm around Amy's shoulders. "Come on, Amy. I'll walk you home. It's not far."